HOW

THE END

OF THE

WORLD

Books by Tom Mitchell

HOW TO ROB A BANK

THAT TIME I GOT KIDNAPPED

ESCAPE FROM CAMP BORING

WHEN THINGS WENT WILD

HOW TO STOP THE END OF THE WORLD

HOW TO STOP
THE END
OF THE
WORLD

TOM MITCHELL

HarperCollins *Children's Books*

First published in the United Kingdom by
HarperCollins *Children's Books* in 2024
HarperCollins *Children's Books* is a division of HarperCollins*Publishers* Ltd
1 London Bridge Street
London SE1 9GF

www.harpercollins.co.uk

HarperCollins*Publishers*
Macken House, 39/40 Mayor Street Upper
Dublin 1, D01 C9W8, Ireland

1

ISBN 978-0-00-859714-6

Tom Mitchell asserts the moral right to be identified
as the author of the work.

A CIP catalogue record for this title is available from the British Library.

Typeset in Plantin by Palimpsest Book Production Ltd, Falkirk, Stirlingshire

Printed and Bound in the UK using 100% Renewable Electricity
at CPI Group (UK) Ltd

To Ethan and Jensen

CHAPTER 1

For Col Coleridge, the annual Westerham and Sevenoaks family athletics day was like a visit to the dentist. Not only did it happen too regularly, but it was also . . . well . . . like . . . the worst thing ever. Okay, so not the best comparison, but figurative language is difficult when you're blinded by passion, and Col *really* hated both orthodontics and field events, with a strength equalled only by his feelings towards screen-time limits. It's not like his mum and dad ever set *themselves* screen-time limits.

And, I have to say, I completely agree. (About the running. Screen time *is* a worry.) Because how can running be 'fun'? You don't see any animals doing it for the lolz. Antelopes don't start giggling when they're being chased down by lions. Consider this: have you ever seen a jogger smile? No. Case closed. I've never trusted anyone who claims to like running. But, unlike me, Col's parents didn't, *couldn't* understand his attitude. It was as if they spoke a different language to their son, ran on an alternative operating system.

The headline event of the Westerham and Sevenoaks family athletics day was the family relay race. Each family member held a baton and ran a certain number of metres that Col could never exactly remember, but was loads, literally hundreds, and then handed the baton to the next family member. Showing a complete lack of imagination, the winners were the first to cross the finish line. That was another thing Col didn't like about sports. They were always so . . . predictable. Not like games. At least his Xbox had the power to surprise.

Relay teams were meant to comprise four runners, but, as Mum had complained that this was prejudiced against one-child or single-parent families, Dad was allowed to run twice – at the start and at the end. Col was, therefore, third.

That *fateful* day, he wore his special sports watch. A birthday present, it was a strangely pale blue, like it was ill. He hadn't asked for it, but had still tried to appear grateful because he was a GOOD BOY. In addition to showing the time, a genuinely useful feature, the watch could take all kinds of health readings when you were out being healthy. Col tended not to wear it, though, because the constant alerts that it was 'time to stand up' got a bit annoying.

And so he stood behind a line in his lane, the running track being a wonky set of squished and massive circles painted on to a local field more accustomed to dog poo and teenagers on quad bikes. Behind them were farmers' fields and beyond these Tower Wood.

Col picked out his dad, lined up across the other side of the looping track. He was the only competitor to have adopted a runner's crouch rather than standing normally (because, you know, this wasn't the Olympics). There was no starter's pistol – something else that Col's mum had complained about – just a woman, whom Col had seen earlier wearing a T-shirt with the slogan *If I collapse, please pause my watch*, with a really loud voice, who shouted, 'ON YOUR MARKS, GET SET, GO!'

Barely a second had passed before Dad was well ahead of the pack. By the time he'd reached Mum – who, with her specialist knowledge of baton-passing technique, had already started a slow jog – he was about a bus-distance away from his closest rival, a girl Col's age.

Baton successfully passed, Mum speeded up, her legs a blur of motion. It was now that Col's body began to move. Not his legs in a slow jog, as he'd been repeatedly instructed to do by both parents throughout the past week, but instead his stomach, in an urgent cramp. It felt like it had shrunk to the size of an apple and was desperately trying to swap places with his heart. But his heart was having none of it and displayed its own displeasure by beating ten times its normal speed. His watch vibrated an alert, but he dared not look in case it suggested he call an ambulance.

Mum had turned the bend and was rushing down the straight, like a Lycra flood, towards Col. Now *really* was the time to start moving. The kindly parent in the lane to his left, up ahead, said as much.

'I know,' said Col. At least that's what he'd intended to say. What emerged was more like '*gagalagawa*'.

'Go!' shouted Mum, now but a car's length away from Col, her arms furious pistons, the baton cutting through the air in brutal stabs. Her face was tight and strawberry-red and in no mood to be dealing with Colin being Colin.

And Col *did* want to go. And Col *did* want to win the

race. And, if he'd taken the baton and *walked* to where his dad waited, the family would surely have done so.

'Col!' shouted his father from his position round the track, the word sounding like a baby's scream (a really angry baby).

Mum was so close that Col could smell her breath.

He wanted to move. The only problem was that his legs didn't. They could have been made of wet sand for all the use they were to him.

Mum could have continued running. She could have dodged round her son, missed him out of the relay altogether, and handed the baton directly to Dad. She didn't, though. Had she thought Col might break into a sprint at the last minute? Mothers are forever optimistic. They have to be. Alternatively, she could have stopped. She could have asked Col if he was okay, and why he was gurning in that ridiculous way.

But, whatever she was thinking, she didn't stop . . . not until she'd collided with Col, knocking him to the grass with an 'oof', and landing on top of him in a barrage of sweat and sportswear.

'Ow,' said Col. 'My bits!'

'First-aiders to Lane One!' shouted the woman with the loud voice from the other side of the track.

Col's mum was sharp and bony, all elbows and knees digging into the soft parts of her son's body. But this wasn't the greatest pain. The greatest pain, burning like a star in the centre of Col's skull, was the knowledge of what would surely follow: a telling-off.

CHAPTER 2

'Were you trying to be funny? Was that it? You know, Col, there's enough going on in the world at the moment without having to worry about you.'

'She's talking about climate change,' said Dad. Mum nodded. 'And double-digit inflation.' Mum nodded again. 'And global inequality.' Once more, Mum nodded. 'And the riots in—'

'Phil!' said Mum. 'We get it. The point is we can do without Col acting up.' Her voice changed, from strained to pleading. 'You know how much we love the annual Westerham and Sevenoaks family athletics day, Colin.'

She limped. She was definitely doing it for effect, and Col was trying his best *not* to feel guilty. Fine. She'd sworn when Dad had pulled her off Col, something he couldn't remember having heard before, but it hadn't really been *that* violent a collision. She'd turned her ankle, she'd claimed. People, we've *all* turned our ankles. I did so only last week, during a regrettable incident outside a sushi restaurant.

'And so not only do I have the indignity of today's incident,' continued Col's mum, 'but I'll also be off running for *weeks*.'

Col could tell things were serious because Mum didn't normally speak like this, her words hot and indignant. In contrast, Dad had seemed muted, like someone had turned down his personality's volume. And, as his mother limped, Col walked. And Dad talked.

'Did you see how far ahead we were?' he said with a sigh. 'You could have walked it, son. You could have walked it.'

'It's so important to be active,' said Mum. 'You don't understand now, but you'll be thanking us when you're our age. We're doing this for you. I'd take a thousand ligament strains if only you would understand.'

Col felt like saying that the amount of pain she was in (exaggerated or not) suggested that being active was not only overrated but also dangerous. He didn't, though. Conversations like these came round about once a month, which corresponded pretty much to the regularity of his sporting disappointments. If he played the conversation well enough, it'd be over by the time they reached home and, depending on how satisfied his parents were with his assurances, he might even be able to get on his Xbox before dinner.

His parents were annoying, but they weren't monsters.

'Fit body, fit brain,' said Dad.

'It's healthy body, healthy brain,' snapped Mum, grimacing.

'Same difference,' said Dad. 'And anyway, Col, we're not expecting you to run for Kent or anything like that. We only want you to take an interest. It's like school. Nobody *wants* to go to school, but once you're there it's fun.'

'I don't mind school,' said Col, thinking this was a decent opinion to offer. And he wasn't even lying.

At school, there were loads of adults, and only one ever got on his case about being active, and that was his PE teacher, which was fair enough because it was literally his job.

'We know you don't, son,' said Mum, her tone changing to a weird, almost pitying one.

'And we've warned you before about your Xbox,' added Dad. 'You spend too long on it.'

'It keeps my fingers active,' said Col. 'And develops my hand-eye coordination.'

'I'll give you hand-eye coordination,' said Dad, intending it to sound like a threat even though it made no sense.

As Mum launched into the familiar speech about how she'd once received a promotion at work because her boss had seen her running and had been impressed by her tenacity (whatever that meant), Col noticed something: there were strange markings on the pavement.

At first, Col assumed they were some bored kid's attempt at tagging. Westerham was close enough to London for locals to act like they lived in the big city, but distant enough for their efforts to be incredibly lame. Take, for instance, the 'gang' that hung out on the playing fields at night. They wore hoodies and smoked vapes, but Col knew for a fact that they all attended the local independent school. One of them was even called Algernon, which was a name that Col would swap for his in an instant, but didn't suggest the mean and edgy street life of South London.

But this wasn't the work of kids. There was something about the marks that was too . . . arty, too . . . mysterious. Tags were normally a recognisable word or a name. 'Eggs', for instance. Or 'Adz' or something like that. No, these weren't tags. They *were* something, but just what exactly wasn't clear. Like grainy footage of UFOs, if that makes sense. It's difficult to describe.

The shapes had been drawn on the pavement in thick chalk, mostly white, but also blue and red. Were the different colours significant? The United Kingdom? Col hoped it wasn't to do with politics. There'd been too much of that recently.

There'd be groups of the markings in a row, then suddenly none, then maybe one or two, and then another cluster. It was difficult to see how the pattern made sense. Some of the symbols had faded with time; others looked fresh.

'So do you have anything to say for yourself?' asked Mum. 'Before we get back home?'

'I had a panic attack,' said Col quickly. 'It happened

to Jake in school, and his hands just froze, and he couldn't eat his sandwich because it was tuna.'

'*What?*' said Mum.

'He's terrified of fish. Something traumatic happened at a Sea Life birthday party.' Col paused for a second before attempting to change the conversation. 'You know, in Brighton. Anyway, what do you think all these markings on the pavement mean?'

'Listen to your mother,' said Dad. 'Pay attention. Because, in another reality, we three are walking home with gold medals round our necks. And I'm treating you all to a Nando's because Nando's are for winners. Do you know how long I've been looking forward to the relay? It was something to do as a family.'

(The one time they'd been to Nando's, Dad and Mum had both asked for 'extra mild' spiciness. Which, in terms of characterisation, is all you need to know, really. And makes my job incredibly easy.)

'They wouldn't have given us medals,' said Mum. 'They couldn't even organise a finishing tape.'

'Okay,' said Col. 'I'm sorry. Mum. Dad.' Another brief pause. 'So what *do* you think these markings are?' He tried to change the subject again, hoping that repetition might help, pointing at another row of symbols. Their chalk was bright so they couldn't have been old. 'There's *loads* of them.'

'Are you taking this seriously?' asked Dad. 'Forget the pavement. Remember what we said about boarding school.'

'Which is too expensive,' said Mum firmly. 'But there are weekend sports clubs, holiday sports clubs, targeted at kids like you. I've seen them online. Train the Pain.'

Parents should be banned from the internet. Really they should.

Finally they arrived outside the family home, and, with a long sigh, Dad put his arm round Col's shoulders.

'Our problem,' he said, 'is that we love you too much.'

'We just want the best for you,' added Mum. 'What happened today, Colin? What's wrong?'

Col shrugged. He didn't know. He really didn't. Maybe they thought – and you too – that he'd been trying to be clever by saying he'd had a panic attack. But he hadn't. It was the only way he could explain his paralysis. You put too much pressure on anything and eventually it'll break. Like the shatterproof ruler that had lasted only two weeks of Year Seven.

'My legs wouldn't move. I'm sorry. I don't know what else to say.'

Mum ruffled his hair. Dad let his arm fall from Col's

shoulders, then cleared his throat like he was about to speak. But he didn't. Instead there was a period of awkward silence. Right there. Outside their house. When it became too much, Mum couldn't help but talk.

'Broadband,' she said.

'What?' said Dad and Col together.

'They're installing superfast broadband. The markings must have something to do with that. We had a leaflet through the door. Apostrophes all over the place.'

And Col didn't even have to ask.

'If you get more active, I promise we'll sign up for it,' said Mum with a sigh.

'Liz!' said Dad in protest. 'I don't think we should be encouraging his gaming.' There was a pause. 'But, having said that, have you noticed how laggy the peloton gets recently?'

Col didn't engage. He didn't believe the chalk symbols had anything to do with broadband. There was something sinister about them. As if they were a code. As if whoever had made them was trying to hide the reason why.

CHAPTER 3

Col's parents were both solicitors, but in rival offices, if you can believe that. They worked very hard, which Col didn't mind because this meant that in the summer holidays he had most weekdays to himself. Okay, so there were always chores – set, Col suspected, because his parents resented him getting to spend the day doing 'nothing'. But, apart from these jobs, the days opened up like the sea. A void to be filled with . . . gaming.

Next door lived a boy who was a year younger than Col. His parents seemed normal – that's to say they weren't obsessed with sport. The boy, however, was. Very much so. It was as if the two children had been swapped at birth. And if it weren't for Col having the same large nose as his dad, *and* the fact that the boy next door and his family had only moved from Dorset eighteen months ago, they might well have been.

Next-door Noah wasn't into *normal* kids' sports, though. Col could have dealt with a footballer or a tennis player or even a cricketer. He'd have coped with someone who spent their time throwing a ball into a hoop. But Noah, and even *I* shudder as I write this, was into . . . golf.

'It'll serve him well when he's working in business and looking to network. That's where deals are made, son, out on the golf course,' Col's dad said whenever Col laughed at the idea of knocking balls into holes and calling it a sport.

Sure, every human activity can be reduced to its bare essentials and made to sound ridiculous. I think this is mainly because everything we do *is* ridiculous. Col had enough self-awareness to realise that this was as true of fighting Xbox dragons, say, as anything else. But golf, especially when a kid is doing it, was obviously more ridiculous than anything else, and definitely any other sport.

(Don't @ me.)

Noah practised not by hitting a small ball into a tiny hole, but by smashing a small ball into a massive net that extended across the back of his garden. Given the number of balls that ended up over the fence, though, Col didn't think that Noah was that good, despite the hours he invested.

Why are we discussing Noah? Why did he bother Col so? Well, the Coleridge house was more back to front than your conventional layout, meaning the kitchen was close to the front door, and the living room, with its TV and Xbox, was at the rear. And if you were gaming and Noah was in his garden hitting balls, you could *so* hear it. Now I know what you're thinking. Firstly, how annoying could that possibly be anyway? Well, *very* is the answer, if you were Col. And, secondly, why didn't Col put on headphones like anyone else would? Sometimes he did. But it was almost more the *knowledge* of the sound than the actual sound that wound him up. He felt, despite knowing this to be ridiculous, that Noah was rubbing it in, almost like he was saying, 'Look how active I am!'

And so, on the Monday after the relay-race incident, and before settling down to a solid gaming session, Col made sure to check from the bathroom window – which gave a perfect view over the neighbouring garden – as to whether Noah was out or not.

It was twenty past nine. Col was meant to put the

rubbish outside before half past. And Noah was not in his garden. But a man and a woman in high-vis jackets were. And they were doing *something*. And this *something* included standing over a very strange-looking machine.

'Suss,' whispered Col and completely forgot to brush his teeth.

The only reason he didn't instantly call the police was a) as we've established, he didn't like Noah, and anything that meant his neighbour wasn't hitting golf balls was okay by him, and b) the two potential burglars were wearing high-visibility jackets, which would be a strange choice of outfit for a burglar because, while Col didn't know much about breaking and entering, surely successful burglarising would depend on keeping a low profile?

On actual tiptoes, a little painfully, Col left the bathroom, descended the stairs, crept through the living room, with its curtains still drawn, past the Xbox, and entered the conservatory.

'Conservatory' was what Col's parents called this space, a grand term for what was essentially some wood and a load of glass bolted on to the back of the house. It contained an old sofa and Dad's posh exercise bike, a stack of Mum's fitness magazines with titles like *Active*

Lady and *Fortitude Monthly*. They liked to talk to strangers about their 'conservatory', Col had noticed.

Inside, our hero kept low, hiding behind the exercise bike. He could see the heads and shoulders of the mysterious couple across the garden fence. Turned away from him, they bobbed like ducks. He couldn't hear very much through the glass, only a vague mumbled conversation.

Were they . . . golf inspectors? And, if so, what *was* a golf inspector?

Col crept to the back door that led to the garden. On his knees, he raised a hand and pulled at its handle. Locked. He yanked hard, in the annoying way you always had to when unlocking it, and turned the key that was always kept in the lock, which was, actually, a security concern that Col had raised with his parents on more than one occasion.

The mechanism clicked in a way that couldn't have been that much quieter than a slammed car door. Col dropped his head, paused. He felt his heart racing, and two thoughts occurred to him: his parents would be proud/it was a shame he wasn't wearing his watch. After he'd counted thirty Mississippis, he dared look up. The two strangers were still there. And they *weren't* looking in his direction.

Gently he pushed the door and slipped into the garden. Instantly he could hear chat, gruff like Monday mornings.

(Swearwords have been replaced by the names of birds to protect the reader's innocence/as demanded by my publisher.)

'Of course I've turned the starling thing on, you chaffinch. I'm not a starling idiot.'

'Well, you do a starling good impression of one.'

'Oh, starling off, you giant coot.'

'You wait until Draco hears about this. She'll be angry.'

'I don't give a parakeet about Draco.'

During this offensive exchange, Col slipped closer to the fence. It wasn't high, but was solid, made from those classic slats of wood that would give you an instant splinter should you ever touch them. It also had a number of holes, made from absent knots, and it was through one of these that Col watched.

Their machine looked like a weapon on wheels, an upgradable piece of kit from an old-school first-person shooter. But the couple weren't rolling it about and neither did they have Noah, or his family, tied up. Looking more closely, Col wondered whether it was a lawnmower. Yes, that was how best to describe it: a weaponised lawnmower. It was yellow and black, and where the blades might be located there was a thick box like a car battery. Above the handles, which were pretty much regular lawnmower handles, to be fair, was a screen. The sun reflected against its glass.

'Give me a chaffinch go,' said the woman and shouldered the man away.

Both were thickset, with weirdly wide shoulders, strong in a crushing-metal kind of way. They looked like Vikings. The man had long hair tied back in a rough bun, and a beard. The woman was his female equivalent – she could have been his sister – but had no beard. Even through the high-vis jackets you could see they had thick muscles, the sort you might get from spiriting away seventy-inch flatscreen TVs from unguarded houses maybe.

Col took his eye from the hole. He blinked a bit. To his left was the side gate that opened on to the street. If what he was about to do went terribly wrong, that would be his escape route. Because he had to do *something*, despite how much he enjoyed doing *nothing*.

'Local boy foils Viking robbery': even Mum and Dad would be proud.

He stood. And, as the two suspected burglars still had their backs to him, he was forced to clear his throat to get their attention.

'All right,' said the man, hardly pausing from trying to get their machine to do whatever they wanted it to do: plant mines or mow the lawn. Still, Col's presence appeared to have stopped the swearing. 'Look. You press this.' The man jabbed a finger at the screen. 'You've not even turned it on. I told Draco it was a mistake to have you partner me. You're not tech literate.'

'What are you doing?' asked Col, his voice not shaking even a little bit. It was weird. It didn't even feel as if it was him speaking. It was more like he was watching somebody else, somebody . . . confident. A video-game character?

The woman looked up from the screen. She smiled. At least that's what Col interpreted her strange baring of teeth to mean. She could have been growling or suffering from a loose filling.

'Broadband,' she said. 'We're installing broadband. And we're very busy. Thanking you.'

'Very busy,' said the man. 'Thanking you.'

They returned their focus to the screen.

'There!' she said. 'It's on. It's doing something! What's that percentage mean? Is that a flashing hamburger? Why is there a flashing hamburger?'

'It's not a hamburger. Why would there be a hamburger? It's a battery symbol.'

'What type of broadband?' asked Col.

'What?' replied the woman, not turning.

'What type of broadband?' asked Col again.

'Superfast broadband,' said the man. 'Like really fast.'

'How fast?' asked Col.

Obviously, at this point, the man had identified Col to be a *problem* and so approached the fence. And he *really* did look like a Viking, more so the closer he came. It wasn't just the beard, the hair – it was the way those broad shoulders rolled as he moved. He pointed at Col's house. 'Like I said: superfast. And we request that you go back inside and leave us alone to do our job now, thanking you.'

Col noticed a tattoo on the man's wrist. It appeared to be a symbol, similar, Col realised, to the chalk symbols he'd seen. The man saw Col looking and dropped his hand.

'Are you the ones who've been making those markings?' asked Col. 'The ones on the pavement?'

'We don't have time for this,' said the man.

'Ross, stop gassing and get back here. I think it's out of battery. The burger's flashing again. How do you charge it?'

But Ross didn't do as he was told. Instead he stared at Col. It wasn't a stare you'd expect from a broadband engineer. No. There was too much suppressed violence for that. Col took a step backwards, out of the man's reach.

'Don't use my name in front of civilians, Susie,' said Ross from between gritted teeth, still staring at Col. 'Remember?'

'You just used mine!' said Susie, distracted now from the screen. 'You really are a hulking idiot. You didn't even charge the machine.'

'It's not my job to charge it.' Ross spoke to Col. 'Why don't you run along, son? Before you get yourself in trouble. Big trouble. The adults need some adult time here.'

'What speed broadband are you installing? I'll get my dad to buy it. Is it really fast? Like three megabytes a second?'

(Col's broadband was always lagging and far from the best available, and even his was thirty mbps.)

'How about *six* megabytes a second?' said Ross, who also attempted something resembling a smile, which, like his partner's, completely failed, making him appear more constipated than happy. 'You like that?'

'Okay, bye then!' said Col and wandered, quite quickly – a quick wander – back into his house.

It was an Oscar-winning performance because he didn't run. Sometimes effective acting is simply moving slowly. He even closed the back door – locking it, of course – as if his biggest care now was what to have for lunch. But as soon as he was out of sight he sprinted. Through the living room, up the stairs, straight through to his bedroom and to his phone.

And, for the first time in his life, he dialled 999.

Excitement overload, bozos!

CHAPTER 4

A little under an hour later, Col was sitting in the living room with his dad, back from work and not happy, and two police officers, still at work and also not happy. One of the officers was jammed awkwardly alongside Dad on the sofa. Shoulders uncomfortably close, they faced Col and his armchair. The other police officer leant self-consciously against the wall. Col had offered her his seat, but she'd replied that she didn't think it appropriate.

'And then there's the call handler, and the time they might have spent responding to genuine emergencies instead of talking to you and—'

'I thought they were committing a crime!' said Col, but not as loudly as you'd have hoped.

The seated police officer looked shocked to be interrupted.

'Col!' said Dad. 'Mind your manners, young man.'

(This was the first time that Dad had ever called him 'young man'.)

Initially Col acted the same way any of us would when faced with police officers in our living room. I'd be intimidated. I'd be quiet. And so was he. He looked at the carpet and its many ghosts of stains past. These officers, with their radios and stab vests, could take him away if they fancied it. Lock him up good and proper. No food or Wi-Fi for days. Enforced exercise.

But the more they wanged on about Col wasting their time and how the high-vis Vikings were only broadband engineers, the more he felt a bright star of resentment grow within his chest. It was a strange feeling. It was close to . . . *caring*.

'I thought they were burglars. They were swearing and acting like burglars.'

'Burglars break into houses,' said the standing police officer who, up until now, had left much of the talking to her partner. 'They don't hang around in gardens wearing high-visibility jackets.'

She made a fair point. But there was something to

her voice, a kindness to her eyes, that suggested she wasn't as hot for this telling-off as the two other authority figures on the sofa. And so Col directed his pleading at her.

'They didn't look like broadband engineers. They looked like Vikings! You saw them, right?'

'Col!' warned Dad. 'We don't judge people by their appearance.'

'No, I don't, but . . .'

The female police officer smiled. 'We can hardly go around locking people up for having beards, can we? And being a Viking's no crime. Sadly. Not any longer.'

Col tried to sound rational. 'I asked them about the broadband speed, and they didn't know what they were talking about. Did you see their ID? Do you know for sure they're who they say they are? I'm a concerned citizen.'

Any other dad might have been proud to see their son stand up for themselves. But not this one.

'I'm warning you, Col!' he said.

'Their machine,' Col pleaded, almost willing the policer officers to telepathically understand that he had a point.

'GPR,' said the police officer next to Dad. 'Ground-penetrating radar. They use it to check underground for pipes and cables.'

'But—'

Dad snapped. 'Go to your room.' He paused, turning to the police officer alongside him. 'Is that okay?' The police officer nodded. 'I'm meant to be in a meeting with an important client right now. Do you understand, Col? You're costing me.'

He only ever seemed to be with important clients. Were there ever any that weren't significant? Or any moments in the day when his dad wasn't in a meeting?

As Col slowly climbed the stairs, he heard one of the police officers speak.

'You won't believe the amount of crime there's been these last twelve months. It's like the general public are on something.'

'They *are* half the time,' said the female police officer.

'If only we were on . . . commission,' said the man.

'Yes! Commission! Good one,' said the woman, and Dad gave a fake laugh.

After the police left, Dad didn't bother coming into Col's room. He just shouted up the stairs.

'Don't leave the house. You'll have a ton of explaining

to do when your poor mother gets back. *And* you never took the rubbish out.'

The front door slammed. Col rolled from his bed, stepped across his sock-strewn floor, and stood to the side of the curtains. Pulling an edge back a little, he watched Dad get into his car, a bright red BMW 5 Series. The man was incredibly proud of this car. *Incredibly* proud. After waiting for a girl, around Col's age, on a bike to pass, he pulled away with a roar of acceleration that was hardly needed but, I'm sure, was done for Col's benefit.

Col remained at the window for a while, not thinking about much, really, but feeling all kinds of miserable. And then he noticed something outside: a new chalk marking on the pavement in front of Noah's house. The same two symbols as before.

Maybe it *was* to do with broadband.

But, then again, maybe it wasn't.

CHAPTER 5

'Mum. Dad. I've decided to take up jogging.'

Col's parents were sitting at the kitchen table, eating porridge and reading the ever-depressing news on their iPads. Obviously they were shocked by Col's announcement. It was unclear, however, what they found more disturbing: that Col was up before eight or that he was wearing sports gear.

He pointed at his wrist. He was wearing the pale blue watch.

'I found a blood-oxygen function.' Col's voice dropped. 'Whatever that means.'

'I nearly choked on my porridge,' said Dad, his face almost the same colour as the watch, as Mum gave his back a sharp slap.

It had been the Viking's tattoo that had persuaded Col that he was on to something. Mum's telling-off, when she finally got home, hadn't been as bad as all that and, actually, showed some sympathy for the idea that calling the police when you suspect a crime to be taking place wasn't entirely inappropriate. In fact, she seemed more angry about him not taking the rubbish out. Anyway, after she'd said her bit about getting out of the house more and keeping his imagination under control, Col had come up with the amazing tactic of suggesting they take away his Xbox until he proved he deserved it back. Given that they'd have confiscated it anyway, he didn't consider this losing out.

A gambit is a chess opening in which a player sacrifices material with the aim of achieving a subsequent positional advantage. (Wikipedia)

(Maybe the two sessions of Mr Castle's Chess Club that Mum had bribed Col to attend hadn't been a *complete* waste of time?)

'And it's *running*,' said Mum. 'We call it *running*.'

'Jogging is something people did in the nineties to lose weight,' added Dad, finishing off a slight porridge cough.

'We're *not* in the nineties, and we're *not* trying to lose weight.'

He seemed weirdly angry about this. Or maybe it was the after-effects of the near-choking. Anyway, Col couldn't argue with the facts. Mum and Dad were like pipe cleaners, on the edge of looking like they had a health problem, in fact, in that particular way that ~~joggers~~ runners often do. Have you ever noticed? As if they have an illness, and that illness is exercise.

'Do you have your key?' called Mum as Col left.

'Don't forget to stretch!' shouted Dad.

Col could see Noah in his garden, readying himself for an early-morning session of swinging. *Imagine getting up this early to do that*, thought Col as he closed the back door. *And in the holidays too!* (It didn't count that *he* was up early because this was all part of his *sick tactics* and not because he wanted to be active.)

'Hey,' said Col. This was unusual because he hardly ever said 'Hey', and it was even rarer for him to talk to Noah.

Noah fiddled with the piece of Astroturf from which he struck his golf balls. He'd bring this out especially and place it on the actual, real-life grass that otherwise occupied the garden. The boy looked like a baby badger.

You may think this sounds cute, but believe me it isn't. He was dressed in a golf uniform: polo shirt and chino shorts and a sun visor.

If Noah had been surprised at his neighbour's greeting, he didn't show it. He didn't even look up. This is the mark of an elite athlete: total focus. And it was for the best that he didn't because Col started to 'stretch': doing weird things with his legs that Mum would instantly run out to correct if she were there to witness the horror of it.

'Did you hear about yesterday?'

'No,' said Noah.

'There were strange people in your garden.'

'Is this a golf joke? Are you teasing me about golf?'

'No,' said Col. 'I swear. Two giants in high-vis jackets.'

'Broadband,' said Noah.

In other circumstances, Col might have found the hose and sprayed Noah and then apologised and explained that he'd been trying to water some plants, but it had gone horribly wrong. He'd done this before, and more than once, and it had been *so* satisfying, even though, as I've already said, our Col was a *Good Boy*.

'Did your parents know they were coming?' he asked.

'Yes.'

'How?'

'There was a leaflet.'

'You would've thought they'd email,' said Col, smiling to himself.

Noah steadied his stance, addressing the ball. He stood like a penguin, if penguins played golf. Hunched shoulders, side-on, head dropped. He pulled back the club, lifting it in a sweep behind him.

'Don't you think it's weird?' asked Col.

Noah paused.

'No.'

Noah unpaused.

'They looked like Vikings,' said Col. 'Did I say that already?'

Noah sliced the shot. Instead of a ripple of netting, there came a smashing of glass from the far neighbour's shed. But before Noah could throw accusations of intentional distraction, Col was gone.

Left from the house, the street ended at a junction with the main road. This was the route that Mum and Dad took in separate cars to their offices. Col, therefore, turned right. Because – and this might not be a huge surprise to you – he wasn't intending to go for a jog or a run or a high-intensity interval training session or whatever. He did canter, yes, but as soon as he met the bend in the road, a turn that would prevent anyone from the house seeing him, he slowed.

In truth, he *was* a little out of breath, despite only running for about a minute. Maybe it wouldn't hurt to go for a few walks this summer, he thought. Maybe even find the bike, buried like an ancient artefact, in the tomb of the shed. Sort the chain. Grease the gears.

His plan:

1. *Take pictures of the chalk markings. He'd been working from memory so far. With images, he'd be able to Google like a pro.*
2. *Check they were all the same two symbols. He was 99 per cent sure this was the case, but it wouldn't hurt to be definite. And anyway what else was he going to do? He'd given up his Xbox! Dad had locked it away! Literally. Well, not literally, but—*
3. *Record, if he could be bothered, exactly where the markings were. He thought he'd begin with the few streets around his house. He knew that some spots had more than others, and it was worth monitoring for patterns, he thought, although he wasn't entirely sure why. Could he drop pins on Google Maps? Or something like that?*

Col stood between a house no different from the other redbrick semis (although with a front hedge that could do with a bit of a trim, to be honest) and a battered green Honda. And he stopped there because *here* was the first marking after turning the bend. He pulled out his phone to take a photo and was gently weighing up the advantages of getting back into bed on returning home when a pair of Converse materialised in the phone's camera frame.

'Are you okay?' asked a voice, which, presumably, was linked to the trainers. 'Or do you always look like that?'

CHAPTER 6

'Broadband,' said Col. 'I'm installing broadband. Look like what?'

'You're, like, eight years old? Eight-year-olds can't even install phone apps, let alone networking infrastructure. And you look like you need the toilet.'

'I'm thirteen,' said Col. 'You're the eight-year-old. And I don't need the toilet. I was focusing. On . . . matters relating to broadband.'

It wasn't a particularly convincing comeback. Don't think that Col didn't know that. He was disappointed with himself. She *didn't* look like an eight-year-old. She was about the same age as Col, maybe even older. He felt like he'd seen her somewhere before, but couldn't remember where.

'Okay, so I'm not a broadband engineer.'

'I know what you're doing. You're not even being subtle about it.'

'What am I doing?'

'Taking photos of the chalk symbols.'

'What makes you say that?'

'Because you're pointing your phone at them.'

Col couldn't deny that this was the case. Nor could he deny that this girl had an attitude. I mean, she hadn't even said hello. Neither had he, to be fair, but he hadn't had the opportunity.

'Hello,' said Col, but she only frowned. 'And, anyway, I'm intrigued.'

'Intrigued?'

'Yes. Intrigued. You know, like *really* interested.'

'I know what *intrigued* means, Mr Dictionary. What's your name?'

'Col.'

'Col?'

'Col. It's short for Colin. My parents . . . they were fans of this Olympic hurdler, but you don't want to know.'

She stood with her arms folded. And Col didn't mean to stare, but his eyes took it upon themselves to do so.

It wasn't because of her appearance, although her face, as Mum would say, was striking. Thick dark lashes round eyes that, he swore, were almost as black. And that hair! Dark and thick and tied into a loose ponytail that fell over her shoulder and down her front. Her skin was tanned, like she'd been out in the sun all summer.

But none of that was why he stared. It was more that she looked like she'd stepped out of an old photo album – you know, the physical sort that were popular back when photos were a thing you could hold in your hand. My parents were always showing girlfriends embarrassing pictures of me in them. Anyway, this girl wore a striped top and denim dungarees. Which were flared. If she'd been older and living in some uber-trendy part of London where 'you need a mortgage for an espresso and it's served in a nutshell' (Col's dad), you'd have thought her a hipster. Here she looked out of place, like a lost visitor from another time.

'What?' she asked.

Col found his composure and shook his head to break his trance.

'My parents say they're something to do with broadband, but I think that's—'

She cut him off. 'Wrong?'

'Yeah. I mean, have you seen them? They're everywhere. The symbols. Not my parents.'

She chewed her lip, eyeing Col up as if trying to read his mind.

'I know what you mean. Because I'm *intrigued* too. And I can tell you this for free: they're nothing to do with broadband. So what are *you* doing about them, Colin? Outside *my* house?'

Col explained his plan. It was a strange experience, someone not instantly dismissing his ideas, even though he wasn't entirely sure that she wasn't just *pretending* to take him seriously in order to laugh later. Adding weight to these suspicions, when he'd finished, she appeared in no way impressed. For one thing, she said: 'And that's it? Why so early in the morning? Do you have . . . issues?'

'I'm pretending to go for a run so that my parents don't get suspicious.'

'So that's a yes to the issues, then.' She mimed ticking an imaginary checklist.

And so Col told her about yesterday, about how he'd challenged a pair of Vikings in his neighbour's garden, how they knew nothing about broadband, and he mentioned the tattoo as well. It was this detail that seemed to be the one that convinced her to act.

Col hadn't even got round to explaining what had happened when the police arrived before she announced, 'Wait here.'

And she disappeared into the front garden of her house. Before Col could surrender to the temptation of jacking it all in and returning home, she'd reappeared, pushing a bike. This, like her flared dungarees, looked ancient, almost antique. The handles were weird, folding back towards the rider. And the saddle wasn't really a saddle. It was more like a seat – triangular and made of leather (desperately worn) and with this little support for the small of your back.

'Why are *you* up so early?' asked Col.

The girl shrugged. 'I've got a paper round.' She jumped on the bike. 'I'd offer you a ride, but it might break with the weight of us both. It's not new,' she said. 'Anyway, I'm Lucy. And if you want to see something properly *intriguing*, you should follow me.'

And she cycled away.

Col didn't instantly follow. She continued pedalling, not looking over her shoulder, not calling for him to get a move on, and travelling at a speed guaranteed to upset pedestrians. Sighing, he put his phone away.

And, for the second time that morning, he broke into a run.

His watch vibrated. 'Are you working out?' it asked.

He flicked through its settings and silenced all alerts.

CHAPTER 7

I'm asking you to imagine Westerham as the Milky Way. But, please, think space, not chocolate.

The high street, with the green and the pubs and shops, and the church spire needling sharply in the background, is at the very centre. The spiral arms are the residential streets. Col and Lucy live at the end of one of these spirals. On one side, across farmers' fields, is the motorway, distant enough that you don't have to worry about fumes, but sufficiently close to create a constant noise like a waterfall, but not the kind you'd get on a meditation app. On the other side of the houses are the playing fields. According to Col, this is an inaccurate name for them because there never seems to be much playing going on, unless you count football, which he doesn't.

That morning, though, there were no goalposts because it was the summer and even rubbish footballers' muscles need time off. In fact, because it was still early, Lucy and Col looked to be the only people mad enough to be out. Well, them and the three Viking lookalikes in the high-vis jackets.

I know what you're thinking.

What. The. Chaffinch?

And you'd be right.

Our heroes observed their targets from a broken bench near the netless tennis courts. There was no weird lawnmower today. Instead one Viking held what looked like a metal detector, while another had a shovel over his shoulder. The third had a phone to her ear.

'Weird, right?' said Lucy. 'They were here last night too.'

'Uh-huh,' said Col.

'Are they the same people that you saw?'

'Uh-huh,' said Col, before judging from her salty expression that she expected more. 'The man with the beard for sure. His name is Ross. I don't know about the others.'

Col studied the Vikings, even though watching people had *not* been part of the plan. He turned to Lucy after she'd spent a decent amount of time not saying anything.

Obviously she'd been waiting for him to do this. Before he could speak, she broke into a monotone stream of instructions. He was almost getting used to her unusual voice already, even though he'd never before heard anyone who sounded so bored by everything.

'You've got to find out what they're doing,' she said, staring at him like a cat that wanted to be let out.

'Uh-huh,' said Col again, before realising exactly what she'd just said. He did a cartoon double-take. 'Why me?'

They'd only just met. It was too early in their relationship for her to be ordering him about. Give it a day, at least.

'Look,' she said, raising her voice slightly to indicate that she meant business, 'I'm no good at talking to strangers. People say I've got an attitude.'

She shrugged. It was exactly the type of shrug that people with an attitude might offer.

'Well . . .'

'Real talk: I get nervous and don't know what to say. I'm not really a . . . people person. I think people are overrated. That means that *you've* got to talk to them. You've the skills. You can chat about the weather or whatever.'

At this point, Col wondered whether she'd been waiting

in her front garden for an unsuspecting innocent like himself for exactly this purpose.

'You're doing okay with the talking right now,' he said, and she dead-eyed him. 'It's acceptable chat. And, anyway, Ross – the one with the beard – he'll suspect something if I go over. He'll remember me. And he's not a person you want remembering you. He isn't too wrapped up in the joy of the world, if you get what I mean.'

'Believe me,' said Lucy, 'I do.'

'Also, he's not very nice. And his biceps are bigger than my thighs.'

'Maybe you've just got tiny thighs,' suggested Lucy.

She screwed her face up in serious thinking. Col decided it best not to interrupt, instead looking quickly down at his legs to check their size. Surely they weren't noticeably smaller than you'd expect?

'What's your number?'

'My phone number?'

'No, your *favourite* number.'

And he was just about to say 'seven' when luckily he realised that Lucy was being sarcastic. She pulled out her phone. In keeping with her overall style, it looked like it belonged in a museum. She showed no shame, though, and Col admired that.

'So?' she asked, and he realised that he'd been staring again.

He gave his number. She pulled out some wired earphones, trailing them up and behind the front of her dungarees, then plugged them into the phone. Col looked away as she did all this. He wasn't entirely sure why.

'Okay,' she said, putting one earphone in her ear, disguising its wire with her hair. 'So I'll call you and you can tell me what to say. It has a microphone, so you should be able to hear the whole conversation.'

She was off before Col could refuse and, when she'd reached halfway across the field, his phone rang.

'Hello?' he said as if it could be anyone else.

'We set?' she asked, seconds away from Ross, the huge Viking that Col had met yesterday.

'Uh-huh.'

There was a beat before she continued. 'So what do I say?'

Col couldn't quite believe that only minutes ago he'd been, quite innocently and almost happily, standing outside this girl's house, minding his own business/taking pictures of strange chalk markings. He would never have predicted that the morning would see him not only having to act like a cut-price spy, but also having to script an encounter between two people he didn't know. And, okay, he *was* good at English, but if he were talented enough to be writing scripts he'd be living in West Hollywood and not Westerham.

This, he decided, was what came from being active: trouble.

CHAPTER 8

'Start with *hey*,' Col suggested.

'*Hey* sounds weird.'

'Fine. Say something else, then.'

Lucy was now within hearing distance of Ross, Col's least favourite Viking.

'Well, what? You're meant to be the expert at small talk.'

'I never said—'

He was cut off by Lucy saying hey to Ross. He was the one with the shovel over his shoulder. The response was so quiet that Col was forced to turn his phone's volume to the max, past the warning that it might damage his hearing.

'Hello,' said Ross. 'We're very busy doing important work, so I can't stop. Have a great day. Thanking you.'

He hadn't even turned to face Lucy. Instead his focus remained on the woman with the metal detector. She walked slowly, sweeping the machine from side to side. There was something to this movement that reminded Col of Noah's warm-ups before his golf-ball-hitting.

Lucy wasn't to be defeated, though. She followed at Ross's heels.

'Ask what they're looking for,' suggested Col.

'What are you looking for?'

'We're installing broadband,' said Ross. 'Superfast broadband. And we're mad busy. Super-mad busy.' Did he sound a touch touchy when he added, 'Have a great day,' once more? Yes, reader. He did.

'Say that's cool. Ask if it will enable cloud gaming.'

Lucy did.

'There's an FAQ on our website,' said Ross. 'Stop bugging me. Go read a book, girl.'

'Ask him for the website address.'

'What's the address?' asked Lucy, unable to resist adding 'boy' at the end.

Ross stopped. Ross turned. Even from this distance, Col could see him pointing a finger at Lucy. The man was riled. The next thing Col instructed Lucy to say would be key. She couldn't be confrontational. She needed subtlety. The right words – in the right order – existed, were possible. Col just needed to pull them from the air somehow.

And then: 'Summer holidays, is it?'

This wasn't Ross speaking. It wasn't Lucy either. No. It was worse. It was . . . Old Mrs Milton. From Col's street. Standing right next to him.

'I've been on holiday for ages now,' said Col. 'Thanking you.'

(Language can be contagious.)

'I've been on holiday for ages now,' repeated Lucy. 'Thanking you.'

Col had intended the 'thanking you' to indicate to Old Mrs Milton that he wasn't available for a chat. It didn't work. And if there were *one* person he wouldn't want to run into, if there were *one* person who wouldn't care, wouldn't even notice that he was on the phone, it was her. It wasn't only Col who felt this way. It was the *whole* town. Initially people assumed she acted like this because her husband was dead, that something inside her had broken and never mended. That was until they discovered that Old Mr Milton was alive.

'I'm on the phone,' said Col, grinning desperately.

Daring to look away from Old Mrs Milton, he saw

that Ross was no longer pointing a thick finger, but had dropped the spade and had his hands on his hips, manifesting a level of sass that you'd not think possible from someone with such a wide chest.

'I remember when I was your age,' said Old Mrs Milton in that gramophone voice that only retired people can pull off. 'We didn't have phones. We had to make do with cans tied together with a piece of string. You laugh, but I'm not joking.'

'I'm not laughing,' said Col, who really wasn't. 'I'm on the phone now actually. Sorry.'

'Would you like to stroke Albert?' asked Old Mrs Milton.

Albert, her dog, was currently some distance away, woofing at crows.

'No. Shouldn't you be stopping Albert from doing that?'

Lucy remained with Ross, but was now facing Col, her arms outstretched in exasperation. Smiling at Old Mrs Milton, he put the phone back to his ear.

'No,' he heard Lucy say. 'I don't know who Albert is either. I'm not sure why I just said that. Sorry. Getting back to the digging . . .'

'Albert?' said Old Mrs Milton, looking around, confused.

'Give me a second and I'll work out what I want to say,' said Lucy.

'Sorry,' said Col.

'What for?' asked Old Mrs Milton. 'Have you done something to Albert?'

'Sorry,' said Lucy.

Things were getting too confusing. Col needed to seize control.

'Tell him we know it's not broadband. Ask what they're really doing.'

You could hear the desperation in Col's voice. Well, you could if you were anyone but Old Mrs Milton.

'Albert!' shouted Old Mrs Milton, still at the park bench. 'Leave those birds alone!'

Col looked across at Albert. The dog was still sitting under a tree, barking up at the crows, which had by now wisely moved to the branches. He willed the woman to leave. And although Col's wish came true almost instantly, with more calls of 'Albert!' and not even a farewell, he didn't have long to enjoy the moment of glory because suddenly Lucy was with him and picking up her bike and telling him to run.

'What?' he asked, putting his phone away.

'Just run!'

And, as Lucy jumped on her bike and peddled madly off, Col saw the problem. Ross, the almighty Viking, was sprinting towards them, his tolerance for pesky kids obviously exhausted. He looked like a henchman in a video game – he'll either kill you or you'll kill him – but, given this was real life, *you'd* probably be the one in trouble, to be honest.

And it may have only been the way that he was moving (it didn't look a natural activity for someone whose shoulders were double the width of his waist), but it did seem like he was growling. And was that the ground shaking? Quite possibly. Look, I'm not joking when I say that the man's dad might have been a rhino.

Col jumped up from the bench and started running, heading for the same break in the hedge that they'd entered through, the same spot that Lucy, on her bike, had already almost reached. At least, even if he were caught and ripped in half or whatever it was that Ross might do, he could truthfully tell his parents that he had exercised that morning, something he didn't think would actually happen.

Maybe the crucial element was getting chased.

'Ross!' called one of the other Vikings. 'Give it up! They're kids!'

Col turned round because of this, and that was a mistake. And not only because Ross was within fighting distance. Col, not much of an athlete, as we've established, got his feet in a muddle and hit the turf with a thump. His ankles ached dully, and his chin absorbed most of the impact, snapping his teeth together.

Ross loomed.

Col lifted his head. And there! Look! A bike wheel.

Ross loomed some more.

And Col heaved his chest from the grass. And there was more of a bike. And Lucy too, reaching down to him.

'Quick!' she said. 'Get on!'

He struggled to stand. He struggled even more to get on the bike. As Lucy kicked out a foot to push forward, Col sat on the seat, his arms turned round his back to hold on to the small handle at the saddle's top.

The bike wobbled, creeping forward slowly. Ross was close enough to dive, like a rugby player, in a desperate attempt to grab Col. But, with a desperate push on the pedals, the bike thrust forward, out of the Viking's grasp. Momentum gained, they bounced towards the hedge, and Col dared to look over his shoulder.

Ross was lying on his stomach and shaking a fist.

'If I see you two again, I'll rip your heads off!'

CHAPTER 9

'Here's the thing. I don't want to go into your house. I want to go home. I want to lie on the sofa and eat Oreos. That's what the holidays are for. Not this.'

Col, standing, and Lucy, also standing, but astride her ancient bike, were outside Lucy's house. The street was busier now, with grey-faced grown-ups getting into cars, readying themselves for the morning commute.

'Oreos are full of sugar,' said Lucy.

'I know. That's why I like them.'

Lucy pointed to the symbols on the pavement. 'I thought you had a plan. I thought you were investigating these bad boys.'

'I did. I was. Until you came along and got us chased by an angry Viking. I had a plan before all *that*.'

Lucy looked from side to side. She waited for a tired-eyed man to get into his dusty Citroën before speaking.

'What if I could tell you what those markings are?' she whispered. 'You said you were going to plot where they were on a map. What if I'd done that already? What if I could show you?'

Col, it has to be said, was tempted.

'Really?' he said, also whispering, for reasons that weren't clear to him.

It was already some time since he'd left the house to 'go for a jog'. If Mum and Dad were still home, which was possible, it was stretching believability for him to still be *exercising*.

'I'm not going to *beg*, Colin. If you're interested, you should look at my map, that's all. It's not safe to say more out here.'

'It's Col.'

'Okay, whatever.'

It wasn't like she was going to murder him or anything. And, if she tried, it would be something to tell his mates when school started again.

'Fine. Let's go.'

Lucy didn't move. Instead she pulled back and forth on the brake handles. They squeaked like excitable mice.

'We can't let Dad see you.'

'What?'

Maybe he *would* get murdered. By Lucy's strange father figure. A mad, bad dad. In the attic or something. A werewolf parent. Was it full moon?

'I'll explain everything when we're safely upstairs. It's . . . we have to get there without him noticing. It should be fine. Just don't make a noise. Don't speak. Tiptoe. You know? And don't think it's weird because it's not.'

Col waited as Lucy put her bike round the back. The house looked very normal. Maybe *too* normal. Darkened bricks past the hedge, a small front garden that was more weeds than grass. At the very moment he decided that she was taking too long, and the sensible thing would be to leave, and quickly, the front door slowly opened. Lucy. No murderous dad. With one hand, she waved him forward. The other raised a finger to her lips.

CHAPTER 10

'Why didn't you say I had leaves in my hair?'

At the foot of her bed, Lucy pulled tiny shards of green from her ponytail. Col sat on a sturdy box. If there were a single word you might use to describe the room, it would be 'boxy'. Because there were loads of boxes. Cardboard ones.

'How long have you lived here?' asked Col, guessing the answer would be measured in days.

Lucy stared as if he'd asked whether she thought the moon landings were fake. But Col had only to shift his backside a little for the box to creak/Lucy to work out where his question had come from.

'About a month maybe. Dad and I moved here when my old school finished for the summer. He's . . . very preoccupied.' Col didn't ask about her mum. He wasn't *completely* insensitive. Lucy's eyes scanned the room. 'I'm sure I'll get unpacked at some point. If we don't end up moving again.'

For the first time since meeting her, Col sensed a sliver of vulnerability.

'And . . .'

He wasn't sure where he intended the sentence to go. The single word hung in the air. Was he going to ask why they kept moving? But it wasn't any of his business. If she wanted to volunteer the information: fine. Otherwise . . .

Lucy interrupted Col's train of thought. 'But we're not here for a therapy session.'

She picked out a laptop from a cardboard box at the side of her bed. She opened it, fiddled about a bit, typing and clicking, then swung the screen round so Col could see.

'Runes,' she said. 'The chalk markings are runes. Futhorc runes, to be exact.'

The website that Col was now studying looked like it might have existed for as long as the internet had. There was a snazzy border round the brown-coloured page. In the centre, in a very serious font, was the title 'Anglo-Saxon Runes' and then:

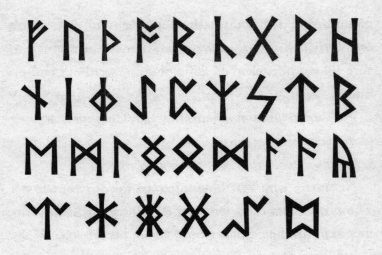

'Wow,' said Col.

Lucy pointed at the two symbols.

'Need mouth?' asked Col, more confused than impressed.

'N and O,' said Lucy. 'That spells *no*.'

'Yes,' said Col. 'Thanks for the English lesson.' He pointed at another symbol. '*Serpent*. That's the tattoo that Ross the Viking had.'

'You're not wrong. And that's not all. Read this.' She pointed at the text on the website.

The word RUNE means secret or mystery. Runes had a religious meaning and were used in religious ceremonies. They were a charm or a spell as well as a way of writing messages.

This is why TO SPELL (meaning to put down the right letters in the right order) and A SPELL (as in a magic spell) are the same word in English. The Anglo-Saxons believed that if you used the right runes, in the right order, they could have magical powers.

'They're magic?' asked Col. 'I'm not sure I—'

'I don't believe in any of that either,' Lucy said. 'But maybe the people we're dealing with do. And that makes them unpredictable. And *that* means they're dangerous.'

Col thought to himself that this had probably already been established, what with the threats of heads being ripped off.

'But what do you—'

She raised a hand. 'Wait!'

She cocked her head. She was listening for something.

'Dad!'

And, yes, she was right. Footsteps. Both kids looked round the room. It was obvious where Col should hide. Lucy pointed at the box he was sitting on.

'Open it!' she hissed. 'Pull out the books!'

Col did as he was told, and then, before he knew it, Lucy's hands were on his back as she pretty much shoved him in, closing the flaps and then sitting on top of the box as her father knocked on her door. In the darkness, Col was curled up and round some very sharp objects and, it has to be said, he wasn't entirely happy with how the day was going. And it wasn't even lunchtime yet.

'Yes?' called Lucy.

'May I come in?'

'Not really.'

Col heard the door open anyway.

'I said *not really*,' said Lucy.

'I didn't hear. Sorry. Do you want breakfast? I'm doing eggs.'

'No eggs, thanks.'

There was a pause. If Col had been able to peer through the walls of his box, he'd have seen Lucy's dad look round the room, and he'd have seen a raised eyebrow too.

'Have you been unpacking?' he asked.

'Yes,' said Lucy.

'We really need to sort that, don't we? We will. It'll be over soon. I promise.'

And, with that, he was gone. Lucy stood up and opened the box flaps. The light came streaming back in, and she held out a hand. Col ignored it as he struggled to get out. She shrugged and returned to the bed and her laptop.

'What is it with your dad?' asked Col, voice low. 'He doesn't seem that bad.'

'You don't know him. I'm a girl. You're a boy. In my room. He wouldn't seem nice in that scenario. And he reads the news too much. It gets him down. But mainly because you're a boy in my room.'

'Really?'

'Really.'

Lucy sighed. She spoke quickly. 'He's mad keen for me to make friends whenever we move, and it's just so cringe, and you don't want him thinking you're my friend because the next thing you know he'll be ringing your parents and . . .' She shrugged. 'You know.'

Col rubbed his neck. He didn't know. But he wasn't going to admit that. And, anyway, it sounded more like *she* didn't want to make friends. Which he could understand. Other people can be a pain. Take Noah, for instance.

Lucy flicked from the website on runes to Google Maps. It was centred on their local area. And it was covered with red markers, a forest of them.

'Every marker represents where I've seen a marking.'

'A marker for a marking?'

Lucy looked up to check that Col wasn't taking the mickey. He nodded earnestly.

'Don't think I've forgiven you for all the stuff on the phone earlier,' she growled.

'Old Mrs Milton is a nightmare,' said Col. Lucy eyed him. 'Honestly.' She continued eyeing him. 'Have you told your dad about all this?'

The eyeing increased to a stare that could curdle milk.

'What do you think?' She zoomed in on the surrounding streets. 'They've marked most houses around here. See?'

'Move along a bit,' he said. 'What about where I live?'

Col's end of the road wasn't quite as busy with red markers. There wasn't one outside his house, and Noah's house was unmarked too.

'That one there,' he said, pointing at Noah's. 'That's where I caught them. And there's a new marking there too. I saw it this morning.'

Lucy added it to the map.

'So this is where you live?' she asked, looking up. He nodded. 'Weird. It's one of the few that hasn't been marked. They've not dug in your garden yet. That's what it means.'

There was a second of thinking time. You could tell Lucy was thinking because she bit her bottom lip and looked up at the corner of the ceiling. With a snap, she closed the laptop.

'I've got a plan,' she said.

'For us?' asked Col, but she shook her head.

'For *you*.'

CHAPTER 11

The difficulty with installing motion-sensitive cameras is that your parents want to know why you're installing motion-sensitive cameras. Also, motion-sensitive cameras are difficult to put up. Especially when they don't come with instructions because Lucy had handed them over to Col from a cardboard box in the corner of her room.

Col spent much of the afternoon attempting to set them up. On his own. They'd agreed this was best. Lucy didn't want her dad thinking she'd got a new friend, and Col fancied having some time to himself. Lucy attracted trouble, mainly due to her saying exactly what she was thinking at any moment, and also because of her habit of making decisions at a hundred miles per hour.

She'd given Col two small cameras. They were white

and plastic, had their own batteries and could be accessed through his phone. They reminded Col of old-style webcams, but Lucy claimed they weren't. Her dad had bought them for their last house when he'd developed a fear of burglars.

'I know how he feels,' Col had replied.

His bedroom looked over the back garden, so he balanced one of the cameras on the windowsill. And, although it took over an hour to get the camera to connect to his phone, eventually it offered a decent view of the lawn. Decent. But not comprehensive. The combination of the angle of elevation and an apple tree meant that the far corner of the garden was hidden.

This was remedied by Col climbing up the apple tree, something he'd not done for five years, after a fall and subsequent arm-break, and wedging the camera between two branches. His first effort was perfect. The app seemed happier with the second camera, and in no time he was watching crisp footage of the earlier hidden strip of lawn, and a crow too.

Back in his bedroom, he sent Lucy a message.

Done.

She replied:

Why the weird face?

He replied:

I was born this way.

. . . which he thought was funny. She didn't reply.

And then Col lay on his bed and doom-scrolled and got annoyed by the frequent alerts sent by the cameras – the 'sensitive' in 'motion-sensitive' was underplaying it a bit. They were set off by *anything*. Not just the cats and pigeons that quite happily moved round the garden all afternoon, but even flies.

It was as he was Googling how to reduce the sensitivity that Dad returned from work. Col didn't rush downstairs to greet his father a) because he'd reached an age where this would be weird, even if he'd wanted to and b) because he didn't want to get interrogated about the morning's run. All kids lie to their parents every so often, Col understood this, but he preferred to do so only when strictly necessary.

Noah and *his* dad must have been waiting for Col's

dad to get home. Because it was *seconds* after the front door opened that the doorbell rang.

'Col!' called his dad.

'What?'

'Come down here, please!'

Nothing about his dad's voice suggested that this was going to be good news.

At the door, as close to the doorway itself as possible, stood Noah and his dad. Col's dad was holding the door open, but looking over his shoulder. There was a change of energy when the three noticed Col's approach. Dad shifted a little, Noah's dad cleared his throat, and Noah stared like he was trying to shoot lasers from his eyes.

'Col,' said Dad as Col joined him. 'Noah here thinks you're spying on him.'

'What?' said Col, spitting out the word, half in shock and half laughing. Dad repeated himself. 'Right,' said Col.

Noah, in his golfing gear, visibly bristled. 'You put a camera up in the tree!'

'Noah says you've put a camera in the tree,' said his dad. For emphasis, I guess?

'Is this true, Col?' asked Dad.

'Kind of,' said Col, pulling his phone from his pocket.

'I *did* put a camera in the tree. But it's not pointing at Noah. I don't know why anyone would want to film Noah.'

'No need to be rude,' said Dad as Noah's father said, 'He happens to be an extremely gifted golfer.'

Why does he always hit his balls over the fence, then? thought Col, fiddling with his phone.

Dad told him to put his phone away.

'I'm showing you something,' said Col, pointing at the screen and its garden camera footage, which was quite obviously pointing inwards, not outwards. Noah and his dad looked at it. Noah's dad shrugged, but Noah was not satisfied.

'He's doing something weird. I know it. I don't trust him. He'll sell pictures of my golf swing on the internet.'

'Why *have* you put a camera in the tree?' asked Noah's dad.

Col looked at his own father before responding.

'I'm meant to be "developing new hobbies" this summer. Mum and Dad don't think I've got enough interests. So I've decided to get into birdwatching.'

There came a pause, something like the brief silence after a nuclear explosion.

'Okay . . .' said Noah's dad, then shook his head. 'I'll tell you something for free: those parakeets are a nightmare.'

Noah cleared his throat. His father understood what this meant and changed his tone. 'Just make sure you don't turn the camera towards our garden. There are laws against that, you know.'

'Give the boy a break, Geoff,' said Dad. This made Col feel very happy, it has to be said.

Goodbyes were offered, and the front door was closed, and Dad waited a moment before saying, 'You expect me to believe you're filming birds? Where'd you get the camera from anyway?'

'I made a new friend,' replied Col. 'When I was out for a jog.'

'Run,' said Dad.

'Run. She's into birdwatching. There's a camera in my bedroom window too.'

'Don't tell Noah,' said Dad. 'And about this run. How did it go? Did you stretch beforehand and afterwards? It's very important to stretch.'

'Yes,' said Col. 'Yes, I did. Lots of stretching. Too much stretching, in fact.'

If Dad didn't believe him, he didn't say. Sometimes,

as a parent, ignorance is preferable. I speak from experience.

'Anyway, have you heard that the prime minister's resigned?' Dad asked.

'Really?' asked Col. 'Why?'

'All kinds of reasons. I'm beginning to think this country's cursed. Have you eaten any fruit today?'

CHAPTER 12

Will I ever fall asleep?

This was the last thing Col thought before he fell asleep. He'd told Mum and Dad that he was tired after the morning's run and wanted to ensure he was fully recharged for another one tomorrow. After getting under his duvet, he'd managed to turn down the cameras' sensitivity. He'd been messaged instructions by Lucy who, to be fair, could do with being a little more patient and a lot more understanding.

And you'll call me as soon as anything happens? she'd asked.

He'd replied with yep and 😐 but this time she didn't query the emoji.

She was probably tired. Col was too, but the idea of

strangers appearing in his garden made it difficult to nod off. He felt a combination of Christmas Eve excitement and the dread of a parents' evening. Things had felt like a game until now – apart from heads being ripped off – and he hadn't really engaged with what he'd do if he caught the Vikings. He couldn't call the police. Not after what happened last time. Could he even tell his parents?

He'd know what to do when it happened. That's what Col told himself. *Yeah. No need to worry. But it'd be weird if they showed up at night. They wouldn't show up at night, would they? Even weird high-vis Vikings need to sleep. It'll be fine.*

A thought: what if they *had* been broadband engineers? He would love superfast broadband. Imagine a future of cloud gaming. He'd never have to leave the sofa. And it *was* a possibility that he'd been the victim of an 'overactive imagination'.

Like that time he'd felt a spider crawl over his foot when he'd been on the sofa, gaming. Because he's not a psychopath, he immediately jumped up and freaked out. The controller had fallen to the floor, and the batteries had spilled out, and the rectangle of plastic that kept them in had cracked and never fitted properly again, but that's not the point. The point is that, in the minutes following the spider incident, Col had persuaded himself that there was a black widow on the loose with a hankering for flesh. Someone at school had once said that their aunt had been bitten by one that had hidden in a bunch of bananas. It happens.

(This was the second-to-last thing he thought before falling asleep.)

He'd been dreaming of nothing when his phone buzzed. An alert. It was a few minutes after one in the morning. Movement had been detected.

And there on his phone, as clear as – well, it wasn't massively clear: the lack of light outside meaning that the footage from the bedroom-window camera was very grainy – were two strangers in the garden.

He gasped. He gulped. He tried zooming in. It didn't work. The angle was poor – you could see all of one's back, but only half of the other's. They might have been digging. There was definitely movement, but what was making it wasn't clear.

Col flicked to the second camera stream. Nothing. A darkness more complete than a broken TV. Nil. *Nada*. Noah. The little loser must have knocked the second camera out of the apple tree. And given the quality of his aim and the fact that the camera was wedged between branches, thought Col, he must have leant over the fence to hit the camera with a putter, or whatever they're called.

Noah would pay. But later. There were more immediate problems now.

Col concentrated on his ears and, in particular, their hearing. Were the intruders speaking? Making any noise at all? The cameras were too cheap to have audio. Ten, twenty seconds passed, and he inhaled sharply and decided that no, he couldn't hear them. It was probably the double glazing. He should have left a window open. Why hadn't he thought of that? Well, because he was a kid on his summer holidays, not a private investigator, that's why.

He considered calling Lucy, but it *was* very late. She'd been clear about keeping on the right side of her dad. And, anyway, he wanted clearer footage before alerting her. He wanted to impress Lucy, but wasn't entirely sure why. If he found something and caught it on film, well . . . that would be perfect. He imagined showing his parents.

'I told you it wasn't broadband.'

Take that!

The side camera was out of action, fine, but if he

opened his bedroom window the footage would benefit from not being shot behind glass.

First off, Col checked that his door was closed. Then he switched on his bedside lamp, but turned it off again immediately, the room flashing a brief second of brightness. He couldn't be alerting the Vikings to his presence. True, they had their backs to the house, but he needed to be careful. It was too late at night to risk being chased again.

He pulled back his duvet. Despite it being summer, there was a chill to the air. He crept to the curtains and stepped into them, as if about to appear onstage. Yes. The strangers were still there. Both on their knees now. And mostly hidden by that apple tree. Not wearing high-vis tonight. There was a flash of light, but they couldn't have been using anything larger than a phone – that's what it looked like.

He'd kill Noah. That's what he'd do. If the second camera had been still operational, it would have filmed everything, no problem.

There were three windowpanes, two narrow ones on either side of a larger central one. The bottom section slid up behind the top section or, if you preferred, the top section slid down over the bottom section. Col turned the latch on the central pane. And, centimetre by centimetre, he pushed it open.

The night drifted into his room – that cool smell of ozone and the sound of the distant engines of lone drivers on the motorway. Col watched for a minute or so. The two figures at the bottom of the garden could have been ghosts. They were silent and remained kneeling. There *was* something hidden by the apple tree, between the left-hand Viking and the fence. Every so often, one of the Vikings would turn to it and fiddle. You could see the movement.

Decision time. A moment when the multiverse, based on what Col did next, would open up in all directions and an infinity of futures. Tell Mum? Tell Dad? That was, maybe, the obvious and even (dare I say) *correct* thing to do. He could still phone Lucy. Or he could confront the Vikings, shouting from his window or even, if he were feeling particularly brave, by going into the garden. He could also do *nothing*. That's always an option. There's a part in all of us that's always tempted, whatever we might be doing, to give up and get back into bed.

Unfortunately Col had an idea. The greater the distance he was able to hold out the camera, the better the angle to reveal what was hidden.

He stepped back from the curtains. The sliver of moonlight that broke through their separating slit was enough to make out details of his bedroom. The desk in the corner covered in last year's schoolbooks. Underwear on the floor. Some lined paper he'd dropped and kept meaning to pick up. The poster of a frog on the wall that he'd had up as long as he could remember. But there was nothing like a broomstick. Nothing like one of those rubbish-grabbers. Nothing long to attach the camera to.

Think! Quick!

He slipped back through the curtains. The Vikings were still there. Don't think that Col didn't know that what he was about to do was stupid. He *so* did. He'd had previous. By this, I mean he'd sat out on the window ledge before. Twice. Once when he was trying to impress a friend (yes, it worked) and once when he was bored.

In Col's defence, whoever designed the house, or at least the windows, had made sitting outside a very tempting proposition. The ledge extended more than you'd think necessary and, in fact, was almost a perfect size for Col's bum. Perhaps it was meant to hold pot plants or a window box.

Col left the camera on the inside windowsill and, careful to make as little noise as possible, pulled his knees up to the window. Then, holding on to the frame for support, he contorted his body to stretch first his left leg and then his right into the night. A breeze penetrated his pyjama bottoms. Also, the window ledge cut into his thighs, so, having grabbed the camera, he shuffled forward to sit comfortably or, at least, as comfortably as you could manage out there in the middle of the night.

Don't look down, he thought to himself.

And that was pretty much his last thought . . .

. . . before the windowsill cracked.

They (adults) say time moves slowly in dramatic moments like this.

But not for Col. Almost as soon as his brain had registered that he was falling, it also noticed he was smashing through the sharp glass of the conservatory below, and that smashing through the sharp glass of the conservatory below *really* hurt. Then that he was no longer falling, but had landed on something, and the landing was a heavy thump and hurt even more than smashing through the sharp glass, but maybe not as much as you'd think.

And then . . . darkness.

CHAPTER 13

Weirdly, Col was back in bed. It reminded him of respawning in a game. A new location, a new life. His first thought, as you'd imagine, was that it (the diggers, the fall) had all been a dream. He even went to check his phone in case he'd missed any camera alerts. But it was as he shifted his body that he realised something was wrong, that *something* being the dull pain he experienced in pretty much every part of his body, including his soul.

'Ow,' he said.

And then alongside the pain came the realisation. He'd not been dreaming. He'd *actually* fallen off his window ledge, smash-bang down through the conservatory. How bad was the damage? To the conservatory, that is, not his body – bones would mend. Col wasn't worried about that.

His allowance was tiny enough already without having to spend the next thirty years paying his parents back. They'd weigh his injuries against the value of the smashed glass. Before deciding how to act in front of them, he'd need to check how much destruction he'd wrought.

Col inspected his hands. Lifting them actually didn't hurt. It was more of an ache, a dull throb round his shoulders. And they looked fine, very much like hands. There were no cuts or anything. He wiggled his fingers. They were all fine too. Full wiggle capability.

Next he checked his phone. His first shock was that it was 11.09 in the morning. And there was a message from Lucy – any news? – and the sharp memory that he'd been crawling about outside to get a better look at the diggers.

Gritting his teeth, Col slipped his legs from under the duvet. His left ankle felt thickly sore (or sorely thick), as if he'd turned it, but there wasn't a bruise or anything. His legs were as free of cuts as his hands. He stood up. Wait, that hurt a bit actually and, worryingly, in a place he'd never felt pain before. Right in the small of the back. He stretched his spine. His bones cracked in protest. His finger followed the stony lumps of his backbone down until it reached the soft spot, and that hurt some more.

Okay. As long as he didn't stretch too often, he should be fine. (The opposite of Dad's running advice.) He limped across to the curtains. He pulled the left one open. This was more difficult than you'd think, and the right side of his body complained.

The window was closed. He released the latch. With his arms shaking and the pain of the effort causing him to sweat, he pushed up the window. He stuck his head out. Below was a Col-shaped hole in the roof of the conservatory.

It seemed a long way down. His right hand pinched the skin on his left hand, just to check he wasn't a ghost. It hurt, and more than it normally would, which was good. That said, he wasn't totally sure that ghosts couldn't feel pain. It would explain why they were always moaning.

He looked at the corner of the garden. It was very empty. What had the diggers done when he'd fallen? Had they helped him? Had Ross been there?

'Why are you out of bed?'

It was Mum. She'd obviously stayed home to look after him. Her face was soft, and she offered an unconvincing smile. Her question hadn't been harsh – more concern than criticism.

'Just trying to keep active,' said Col, although his

heart wasn't in it. 'I'm fine,' he added, getting back into bed. He noticed her face harden a little. 'But I *do* hurt.'

There: it returned to its earlier softness. 'Oh, Col. What happened?'

'I fell out of the window.'

She turned up her tight grin a little. For a moment, she didn't speak.

'We worked that much out. There was a tremendous bang and breaking of glass. We thought the house was being broken into. Your father found you in the conservatory armchair. He thought you'd fallen asleep there. And then he noticed the hole in the roof and the glass everywhere. And . . .' Mum lifted a fist to her mouth. Briefly she looked like she might bite it. 'And he said you wouldn't wake up.' She took a breath. 'We called an ambulance, Col. It took forty-two minutes to arrive, what with the strikes and everything. They said you were fine to stay at home. They said you must have landed in the armchair. They gave you painkillers. It's a miracle you're not seriously hurt.'

She took a step into the room.

'Can I ask a weird question?' Col said, and Mum nodded. 'Was there anyone else around? Was it just Dad?'

'I came down too. What do you mean? I don't understand.'

'I was just wondering if next door dropped in or anything. That's not a joke. Dropped in. I mean came over. Noah, maybe?'

Now nobody likes to upset their mum. (Hi, Mum! Hope you're enjoying this! I love you!) In fact, it's a truth of human existence that there's no worse person to upset. And so Col, having initially been guided by the importance of highlighting how much he hurt, in order to get away with smashing a hole in the conservatory roof, now felt guilty.

'It's okay, Mum. I feel okay.'

Instantly: 'What a year! First the floods, then this! God knows how much it'll cost to repair the damage you caused. Your dad thinks it's structurally unsound—'

Col cut his mother off before she could start talking about pocket-money reductions.

'But if you had an ibuprofen I wouldn't say no,' he said, wincing as he did so (and, in all fairness, he did have quite a sharp throbbing behind his eyes).

Mum shook her head. But more in pity than in anger, and not (just to be clear) because she was turning down his request for pain relief.

'Your dad said something about cameras. About birdwatching. But in the middle of the night? Be honest, Col. I'm not angry with you. Dad is, but I'm not. I just want to know what happened.'

Col lay there and looked at his mother. He imagined what would happen if he told the truth. He imagined the disbelief, the telling-off. This was a moment when surely a slight editing of the facts was acceptable. And anyway it was obvious that she *was* angry with him.

'I wanted to make sure the cameras were lined up for decent footage at dawn,' he said. 'That's when the birds come out . . . to do their thing.'

The words were about as convincing as a lower-school play. He really should research garden birds if he was going to persevere with his cover story.

'I'll get you the tablets,' said Mum quietly.

Col didn't want to spend too long thinking about what had happened or how lucky he'd been in the night so, as at any time that he wanted to avoid thinking, he turned to his phone. Already the stiff pain in his back had lessened, replaced by a dull ache. Maybe this was how it felt to be old? Briefly he felt sorry for his parents.

Before replying to Lucy, he checked the camera app. Expecting nothing, he flicked through the moments before the fall. And yes, one second his back was obscuring the lens and the next it wasn't. But, with the night's single piece of luck, the camera had been left in a position that looked over some of the garden. And so Col had managed to capture the two diggers escaping. And, get this, he'd also caught what they took with them.

A metal detector.

A shovel.

And you're not going to believe this, but being held, cradled like a baby, was a sword.

CHAPTER 14

'Have you read *Jabberwocky?*'

'We're not all weirdos, Dad.'

Lucy's dad ignored his daughter and cleared his throat.

> *"Twas brillig, and the slithy toves*
> *Did gyre and gimble in the wabe:*
> *All mimsy were the borogoves,*
> *And the mome raths outgrabe.'*

Col's mouth dropped open. He shook his head in incomprehension. It hurt to do so.

'It's a poem. By Lewis Carroll. And it does fantastic things with language. I'd often explore it with undergraduates because linguistically the words are invented, but Carroll sticks to the rules of syntax and poetic form. You can infer meaning, you see, through these patterns.'

'It's not time for a lecture, Dad.'

'No, you're right. Not an English literature one anyway,' continued Lucy's dad. 'So *Jabberwocky* is a poem about the killing of a great monster. Carroll wrote most of it when he was staying in Northumberland. They say that it's based on an old story up there about a monster called the Sockburn Worm.'

'It sounds lame, but it's not. Trust me,' Lucy told Col.

'She's right. It wasn't *really* a worm, you see. It was a wyvern. And, umm, a wyvern is a kind of dragon, but with two legs – a snake with wings almost. You often see them on heraldic flags and the like. Lucy, get your phone out. Let's show him one.'

She did, and Col looked at it. And he wondered whether it would be impolite to tell them that his head was really beginning to ache now, and that it had nothing to do with the fall.

Lucy's dad spoke very enthusiastically and wore a brown shirt, a frayed brown suit jacket and, amazingly, a hat – Google said it was a Panama – that middle-aged men sometimes wear when they've forgotten what's cool.

'The Sockburn Worm was not a happy wyvern. It had

it in for Sockburn, a village near Durham. Not only would it kill livestock, sheep and the like, but it would rush into cottages at night and take away children. The beast was finally slain, as legend would have it, by a local knight called Sir John Conyers. But the story doesn't end happily. Conyers didn't survive his battle with the worm. Dying, he instructed his son to bury his body many miles from Sockburn, as far, indeed, as his son was able to travel.'

'He reached Westerham,' said Lucy.

'He did, yes. And the sword that Conyers used to slay the wyvern, a falchion, to be precise – it's single-edged like a sabre – came with him. Which was good because, with his final breath, Conyers also told his son to bury the sword with him, warning that if he were to be separated from it for any period over a hundred years, a second even, then grave consequences – pun intended – would befall the country, if not the world. And that, pretty much, is the story of the Sockburn Worm and Conyers' falchion.'

'You're not a medical doctor, are you?' asked Col. He meant this as small talk but, to be fair, it *did* sound a bit rude.

'Well spotted,' said Lucy.

'I'm sorry. In all this excitement, I've not introduced myself. I'm Doctor Stones. Ignore my daughter.

Sometimes she mistakes sarcasm for personality. And it's so great that she's finally made a friend.'

'Ouch,' said Lucy.

Stones held out a hand. Col weakly shook it.

'You'll need to work on that grip, Col!'

'He's just fallen out of a window, Dad,' said Lucy in her usual monotone.

'I know. I'm joking. It's all very exciting. Not the fall, but the sword. We're on the verge of a great discovery here. That sword – the one you filmed last night – I think that's Conyers'. And it's why we're here. It's why we moved to Westerham. I've been searching for it for the last twenty years.'

'Exposition klaxon,' said Lucy.

You should have seen the look on Col's mum's face back when she'd knocked on his bedroom door and told him he had visitors: a girl who claimed to be Col's friend and her dad who was a doctor, wouldn't you know? Col had nodded like it was no big thing, and Mum had disappeared to fetch drinks and biscuits. They'd arrived approximately five minutes after Col had texted Lucy.

'You moved here because *you* were looking for a sword?' asked Col. 'I know I've had a bang on the head, but I'm confused. You're definitely not a doctor doctor?'

Stones was looking at his phone, trying to find something. He glanced up.

'A Doctor of Literature. But that's not important right now. Give me a second.'

He returned to his phone.

'Tell him the story, Dad,' said Lucy.

'I just did.'

'No, the *other* story. The one that if you'd told me beforehand might have meant I'd have realised what the rune markings were and maybe actually helped you if you ever, like, spoke to me.'

'That's not fair,' replied Stones. 'I *did* tell you. A number of times. You're just very selective about what you hear.' He addressed Col. 'Is she the same with you?'

Col shrugged, which hurt. He was about to say that he'd only met her yesterday, but he wasn't able to because Lucy's dad was holding his phone pretty much in Col's face, which didn't help with his headache, not least because of the full brightness of the screen.

'Is this the tattoo?' asked Stones.

'Yes,' said Col.

'Well,' said Stones, 'in that case, the good news is that I know who's got the sword. The bad news is that, knowing them, we don't have long before they ship it out of the country.'

At this, Col's mother barged into the room with a great rattling of cups and glasses.

'There we go,' she said, offering the tray to Stones, who was sitting on the edge of Col's bed – right, actually, where you might expect a medical professional to perch if they were giving a patient bad news. 'You wanted a black coffee. I'm afraid we're not big coffee drinkers in this house, so it's only instant.'

'That's fine, that's fine,' said Stones, even though you could see by the wonkiness of his face that it wasn't.

'And I've brought orange juice for the kids and some digestive biscuits too. You're all very welcome.'

Col knew for a fact that the main reason schoolfriends were reluctant to come over was because of the digestive biscuits. There were no snack drawers here, no KitKat Chunkies for after dinner, not even a Jammie Dodger.

'Does the orange juice have pulp in it?' asked Lucy.

'Umm, I think it does,' said Mum.

'Then I can't drink it, but thank you anyway.'

Mum froze, her mind paralysed by the straight-talking visitor.

'Lucy! Don't be such a fusspot!' said her father, holding the mug of instant coffee like it contained poison.

Mum leant over to place a glass of orange juice on Col's bedside table. She brushed his hair from his forehead.

'Not a bruise or cut on you,' she said. 'Miraculous.' Stepping back, she fixed Stones with a strange grin. 'So what's the prognosis? The paramedics last night gave him the once-over, but said we had to keep an eye on him for blurred vision or vomiting.' Stones nodded. He smiled. Mum waited. 'So . . .?' she continued.

'Well, that sounds like excellent advice to me.'

'Nothing you want to add?' asked Mum, face thickening with suspicion.

Stones turned to Col. 'Do you feel sick?' he asked. Slowly Col shook his head. 'Is your vision blurred?' Slowly Col shook his head. Stones looked at Mum. 'Sounds good to me! Maybe avoid shaking your head quite so much, though, Col?'

Mum eyed each member of the room in turn.

'I've a Zoom meeting,' she said eventually, and left.

CHAPTER
15

'Once there stood a grand manor house, Lowick Court, at this end of town. Its last owner was a man named Sir Peregrine Amis. Despite the grand name, his origins were humble. He was the son of a blacksmith who'd invented a particularly efficient forge and had become quite rich because of it. Rich enough to send his son to Cambridge. There Peregrine became interested in archaeology. After his parents died and he'd inherited the house, he dedicated his life to finding valuable artefacts that he could display in his own private museum, a grand room, the centrepiece of Lowick.'

Stones was now telling the second story to Col.

'During this point in history, when Britain had an empire that stretched across a third of the world, people, specifically men like Amis, were quite happy to dig up Egyptian mummies or Benin bronzes and send them back to London. Amis's particular interest was a little closer to home, though. He'd heard the story of the Sockburn Worm and the rumoured nearby burial of Conyers. He was known equally among the country's tomb raiders and graverobbers as someone who'd pay well and ask no questions.

'And so one day he was offered a sword by a local farm boy, a falchion with gemstones in the hilt and runes inscribed on the blade, found in shadowy circumstances nearby. The boy told Amis where he'd found it but, soon after, would you believe it, was killed by a kick to the head from a horse. Of course, Amis bought the sword and displayed it in pride of place in his house despite being well aware of the curse – the terrible shadow that would descend upon the world should the sword be parted from its owner for more than a hundred years.

'Amis wasn't superstitious. Despite wanting to believe that he owned the sword that killed the Sockburn Worm, he scorned the prophecy. He even dismissed the belief that the sword is meant to bring great fortune to its bearer, as long as they perform a magical ritual.'

'A magical ritual?' asked Col.

'A magical ritual.'

'Tell him what happens if you *don't* perform the magical ritual, Dad.'

'Not only does a terrible shadow of apocalyptic fate descend upon the world, it descends upon the owner too. Picture the ritual as a test to ensure the owner is worthy of the sword.'

'I don't believe it,' said Lucy.

'And neither did Amis. Weeks after he'd put Conyers' sword on display, his house burned down, and – wait for it – Amis himself was killed. That's the thing with curses. They don't care whether you believe in them or not. His collection was destroyed too – priceless artefacts uprooted from around the world all reduced to ashes. They would have been better off staying where they'd been found. Only one piece survived: the sword. Aware of the curse, but not Conyers' burial place, and blaming it for her father's death, Amis's only daughter did the obvious thing: she threw the weapon into the lake in the grounds. It sank without a trace.

'In time, the lake was filled with the ruins of Lowick Court. The railway came to Westerham, the tracks laid over the estate's gardens. Eventually the trains went away, and houses were built. The motorway. The precise location of the house and the lake was forgotten until recently. The whole story came out when a student of mine found Amis's family papers at his Cambridge college. There was a diary containing his most private thoughts and secret clues. According to Amis, if I'm interpreting the diary correctly, the town church is somehow connected. The answer to the question of the location of Conyers' burial place is there. Perhaps the church *is* the location.'

Lucy butted in. 'The thing I don't understand is why Amis didn't just write down what he knew. Like the exact address even?'

'The man didn't know he was going to die. And it pays to be circumspect when dealing in stolen treasures.'

Col made a mental note to Google the word 'circumspect' at some point.

'You said he exhibited the sword in his private museum,' said Lucy.

'Yes,' said Stones with a sigh, losing patience. It was obviously not the first time they'd had this conversation. 'Not for locals. For people down from London. For *rich* people.'

Lucy shrugged. 'Rich white men more like.'

'Col, I know you're a kid, but haven't you noticed

how terrible the news has been recently? The prime minister has just resigned. The trains are never running. Libraries are closing. And I'm not just talking about Britain, but across the world. Look at America. Col, I believe it's all connected to Conyers' sword. The curse. All of it. And it's not even been a hundred years yet. Imagine how bad it will get!'

As Col remembered what the police had said about there being loads more crime recently, Stones closed his eyes and took a deep breath.

'But all this has come at just the right time. You could say we've been incredibly lucky. As long as we return the sword by the end of the month, all will be fine. We've a chance of saving the world.' His eyes snapped open. 'What do you think? Are you in?'

CHAPTER 16

'Or sell it,' said Lucy. 'We could always sell it.'

'She doesn't believe in the curse,' said Stones. 'And that's fine.'

'I mean –' Col cleared his throat – 'it does sound a bit . . .'

He didn't finish the sentence because he couldn't think of a way of doing so without sounding offensive.

'Fine,' said Stones. 'Forget saving the world, fine, sure, okay, but we can ensure that a dying man's wish, a great warrior too, is fulfilled, and return this sword to where it belongs. Doesn't that sound worthwhile?'

Col lifted his orange juice from his bedside table and took a sip. This summer was turning out to be quite a bit stranger than he'd imagined it would be.

'Technically,' said Col, putting his glass back, 'doesn't the sword belong to me? Or, like, my family? Because, you know, it *was* found in my garden.'

Stones turned to Lucy. 'Look at this boy. Witness the effect of money. His bruises will heal, but his mind will forever remain corrupted.'

'Hang on,' said Col. 'I was only asking.'

'Don't get Dad started,' said Lucy.

'The sword was stolen from its original resting place. Legally, you'd have no claim to it.'

'Right,' said Col, not a little disappointed by this.

'Anyway, the people who took the sword, the ones you and Lucy call the Vikings, they belong to a criminal gang run by an old colleague of mine, a History professor gone rogue. And, believe you me, there's nothing worse. She's called Dr Draco. Which may or may not be her actual name. And she's quite the . . . woman.'

There was a pause before Stones shrugged himself out of whatever memories had caught him. Col was too innocent to realise it, but if you and I had been there we'd have definitely assumed a past relationship.

'Because there's a flipside to the curse. The falchion is also reputed to grant tremendous luck to whoever it's bound to, whoever performs the ritual, which is obviously a double-edged sword, pun intended, if the world's falling round your ears. Knowing Draco, she'll hold on to it until she fails to win the Euromillions, then she'll sell it off. Her gang buy and sell historical artefacts, often stolen. Luckily for us, she also loves historical re-enactments. That's where she finds new recruits. She's persuaded the owner of a ruined castle to host her next one, if you can believe that. The woman should come with a health warning—'

Lucy interrupted. 'Dad and her used to date. Years ago. Before Mum. If that wasn't already obvious.'

(See, what did I say?)

'That's got nothing to do with it,' said Stones, blushing only slightly. 'But, if I know Draco, she'll be unable to resist using the sword in one of her re-enactments. And this is where you two come in. She knows me, so I can't intervene. But you kids can join her re-enactors' society and find the sword, and then we'll work out how to grab it. While you're doing that, I'll finish off at the church and find the exact location of Sir John Conyers' burial site. When all that's sorted, we'll return the sword to its resting place before the world, or any of us, is affected by the curse.'

'Wait,' said Lucy. 'You don't know where we need to

take it yet? Isn't that, like, key to the whole saving-the-world plan?'

Stones cleared his throat. 'It's within five miles of Amis's house. I know *that*. I'm sure it won't take too long to pinpoint exactly where. Clues were left. It's fine. We've got the internet, people.'

Col raised a hand from the duvet, which hurt a bit.

'Why don't you call the police?'

'What will they do? They might arrest Draco and the gang, fine. But the sword will end up in some museum somewhere. Or police custody. And we can't be having that.'

Col's hand remained raised.

'Another question?' asked Stones.

'What about my parents?' he asked. 'Like, shouldn't we show them footage of the Vikings in the garden?'

'No. Because they'll involve the police, and that creates further complications, and we'd never get the sword back in time. Don't worry about your parents. I'll manage them.'

CHAPTER
17

'I have to say,' said Dad, 'this is all extremely strange.'

'Almost unbelievable,' added Mum, cup of tea in hand. 'First, it's running, then it's birdwatching, and now you say you want to take part in historical re-enactments?'

'Don't forget the boy's just had a bang on the head, Liz.'

'The Anglo-Saxon period ended in 1066 with the successful invasion of William the Conker,' said Col, looking at Dr Stones, who gave a pained smile as if Col, despite what he'd told him earlier, should have kept his mouth shut.

'The Conqueror,' he said quietly.

It was a few days after the fall, and they were all sitting in the conservatory. Dad had taped cardboard to the hole in the ceiling because he didn't want any bats getting in. What he had against bats, Col wasn't sure.

Col was almost fully recovered by now, not that there was much to recover from. As his mother kept saying, he'd been amazingly lucky. There was a weird yellowy-black colouring round his left ankle, and it ached a bit if he rotated it, so he'd decided to avoid doing that until the normal colour returned.

The day or so he'd spent in bed had allowed for some deep thinking, and also unlimited access to his phone, despite the way that it amplified his headache.

Did he *have* to go along with Lucy and her dad's plan? Imagine that he turned them down – imagine that he told the Doctor of Literature and his daughter that he didn't want anything to do with rescuing a mythical sword mainly because it sounded absolutely crazy?

But there were still three weeks of the holiday left. With nothing planned. When Col closed his eyes and attempted to visualise what those three weeks would look like, all he could picture was a giant digestive biscuit.

What if he *did* get involved?

1. *It might be fun.*

2. *It would be active, and, even though he still doubted the benefits of being active all the time, what happened at the family relay race was a bit worrying, and Mum and Dad would only make him go jogging as soon as his ankle healed.*

3. *He wouldn't have to pretend to be into birdwatching.*

4. *He could save the world.*

5. *And, most importantly, he'd surrendered his Xbox so it wasn't as if there were anything else to do.*

(He also found Lucy fascinating, in a way he couldn't quite put his finger on, but he was at the age when people started to find other people fascinating in a way that remained incomprehensible for a couple of years, at least. And, even then, most people never got fully on top of the mystery. Trust me.)

And Lucy's dad seemed funny. He reminded Col of someone on TV, but he couldn't think exactly who, and that was annoying. Maybe, if he spent more time in the man's company, it might click?

And there remained a part of Col that still resented

the way the police (and Dad) had treated him after he'd reported the Vikings next door. There's nothing more satisfying than being proved right.

'What happens at a *Dark Ages* re-enactment?' asked Dad. 'I get Civil War or World War Two or whatever because they're playing with guns and doing battles.'

'I just don't know what to believe any longer,' said Mum. 'Honestly.'

'Well,' said Stones.

'Genuinely, I really don't.'

'Liz, this isn't the time,' said Dad.

'And the fact that you're not a medical doctor and, I mean, this whole last week. It's like something out of a book! It's like we're being punished,' said Mum. 'It's like we're cursed.'

The cardboard above their heads flapped slightly in the breeze, and Col tried not to catch Lucy's eye.

'We're not being punished,' said Dad. 'It's just the summer holidays. You know what kids are like.'

'And in my defence,' said Stones, 'I never claimed to be a *doctor* doctor.'

'Living histories,' said Lucy. 'Examples of living-history activities include authentic camping, cooking, practising historical skills and trades, and playing historical musical instruments or board games.'

(Later, when Col checked, he confirmed that this had been lifted from the Wikipedia page on re-enactments.)

'And you want to do that, Col, do you? You want to pluck a chicken or whatever?' Dad turned his attention to Stones. 'I love my son very much, but you don't know him, Doctor. He's never shown any interest in camping, cooking, skill and trades, musical instruments *or* board games.'

'I played the clarinet in Year Five,' said Col, slightly hurt.

'And how did that go?' asked Dad.

'Our son doesn't really have any interests,' said Mum. She stretched out a hand. 'But we love him very much.'

'There is also combat re-enactment,' continued Lucy in her monotone. 'The principal aim of this sort of re-enactment is to recreate historical battles or methods of combat. The variations range from training of historical duelling practices (usually with an appropriate period sword such as an arming sword or rapier and wrestling as a martial art) to re-enactment of historical or legendary battles.'

There was a pause as the adults waited to see if Lucy had finished.

'Okay,' said Mum. 'You certainly seem to know your stuff.'

'It's good clean fun for kids,' said Stones. 'Fresh air and trees and all sorts. And, like I said, I'm more than happy to drive them there and back. It's at Hebdon Castle – you know, the ruins?'

'Never heard of the place,' said Mum.

'Me neither,' said Dad, turning to Mum. 'Next door mentioned a tennis course in Sevenoaks, though, and . . .'

His words worked like a runic incantation, almost turning Col's heart to stone. If there remained any doubt about getting involved, the mention of the 't' word destroyed it.

'Combat re-enactment is incredibly demanding on the body,' said Lucy. 'Good for both aerobic and anaerobic exercise.'

Mum and Dad exchanged glances.

'Well, why didn't you say!' they exclaimed at exactly the same time, in exactly the same way.

CHAPTER 18

Col was unhappy. There were many things that bothered him, as there are many things that bother us all. His appearance, however, wasn't usually something that fell into this category. It wasn't that he was particularly handsome – the way he looked just wasn't something that normally concerned him. The way he saw it was that unless you're stunningly attractive or remarkably hideous, nobody cares. And he's right. But not today.

What led to the change was that on the way to the historical re-enactment, taking place in a field near a ruined castle off the A21, Col had experienced a sudden realisation, a shocking truth that could derail the whole project.

'Ross!' he'd said, the name almost sounding like an expression of pain, which, in some ways, it was.

Dr Stones had swerved a little, jolted by the surprise of the sudden shout during an otherwise quiet journey.

'What?' he'd asked, having resumed control of the vehicle. It was an old car, and not in a vintage, expensive way; more in a windows-kept-from-falling-out-with-electrical-tape way, a scruffy green Honda.

Lucy, in the front seat, had given Col a look over her shoulder that was so sassy it could melt ice.

'You said that the boss got all her henchmen—'

'And henchwomen,' Lucy had added.

'Henchpeople,' Stones had said.

'You said she got them all from the re-enactors.'

'Yep.'

'Well . . . Lucy and me, we've met one. He knows us. He's called Ross. First of all, I spoke to him when he was in my neighbour's garden and then, after that, he chased me and Lucy.'

'Lucy? Is this true?'

'We *were* chased,' Lucy had said. 'But he won't remember us. All kids look the same to adults.'

Stones wasn't sure that this was true, and, even if it

113

was, he didn't want to take the risk. Despite increasing the likelihood that they'd be late, he'd pulled off the A21 and driven to the nearest town, Tunbridge Wells, which Stones had described as nice for some people.

'He means the old and rich,' Lucy had explained.

What Stones had described as a lightning raid ended up taking much longer than planned, so was more like a drizzle attack. There'd been traffic, as there always is when you need to get anywhere fast, and Stones's weird assumption that there'd be a huge and central fancy-dress shop didn't live up to the reality of the twenty-first-century high street.

In short, it was close to an hour after Col's shouting had almost caused the car to crash that they were back on the road, albeit with Lucy wearing a stupid blonde wig ('Just like the princess from *Frozen*,' as the dead-eyed, gum-chewing teenage costume-shop assistant had said) and Col sporting a black beard, attached to his face with pipe cleaners hooked over his ears like the arms of glasses, that was as massive as it was itchy. And, yes, he wasn't happy and, yes, Lucy telling him that he looked ridiculous didn't help.

'Mad ridiculous,' she'd added.

Still, the woman whose face was covered in mud and

also seemed to be wearing a dress made from mud, and who greeted Lucy and Col after Stones had dropped them off at CLASH OF STEEL and made a quick getaway so as not to be spotted, wasn't bothered.

'New recruits?' she asked. 'Come right this way. Nice beard. You were lucky to bump into me.'

Before driving off, Stones had told the kids to imagine they were on a fact-finding mission. All they needed to do was locate the sword and he, as the responsible adult, would formulate the next step. The last piece of advice he offered was, 'If in doubt, play along.' Because of this, Col and Lucy nodded politely and followed the woman away from the car park.

'I think we might be late,' said Col. 'Sorry.'

The woman said not to worry – people were more relaxed about timings a thousand years ago.

They passed through the grounds of the castle, which wasn't really a castle. It was a *ruined* castle, but quite cool-looking actually, with tumbling battlements and everything. Its wrecked walls loomed in the background, a good walk away. Silhouetted against the bright sky, it reminded Col of a broken tooth.

People rushed around like they were busy completing important quests. Most were on their own.

'Do you think her teeth are really like that, or is it part of the act?' whispered Lucy in Col's ear.

Col wasn't able to reply because there suddenly appeared what can only be described as a Christmas tree on legs. And neither of the children had seen anything like it, apart from recognising the tree element and the legs, but separately.

It walked past, in no great hurry, but clearly heading *somewhere*. Which, when you think about it, or even if you don't, is quite unusual for trees.

'Hail, fellows!' it said as it passed. 'Great facial hair!'

Col caught Lucy's eye, and she looked like she was about to laugh. Which was good. Because there was something undeniably unnerving about the walking tree. And not just its accent.

Their guide stopped, and they almost bumped into her back. She turned, and Col pointed at the green figure, who had now paused to talk to a woman in a helmet.

'What—'

'Jack in the Green,' said the woman. 'But don't you worry about him. Harmless. And, I can assure you, not the strangest thing you'll see today.'

She reached into a pouch that hung from her muddy dress belt. Col hadn't noticed either earlier – not the belt nor the pouch – seeing as they too were covered in mud. From the pouch, she pulled a rectangular piece of plastic. Initially Col thought it was a duck whistle (you know, the thing you'd blow to make a quacking noise), but he was wrong. Which, in all honesty, was a little disappointing.

'I didn't know people vaped in the Dark Ages,' said Lucy.

'They didn't smoke cigarettes either, love, which meant they didn't have to cope with crippling nicotine addictions.'

She tightened her focus on the kids.

'So, before we go any further, how about telling me what you two are really up to?' she asked. Smoke rose from her mouth like an escaping ghost.

'What do you mean?' said Col.

There came the oink of a nearby pig, but neither Col nor Lucy dared turn to look at it.

'The beard. The wig. Almost like you're wearing disguises. Well, no, that's wrong. *Exactly* like you're wearing disguises.'

Col and Lucy giggled unconvincingly, in exactly the way people trying to hide something would.

'We wanted to get involved. We thought we were meant to wear costumes.' Col indicated the woman's dress. 'I mean . . .'

'You mean what?'

'Your costume.'

The woman's face reddened in outrage. 'This is no costume, young man! These are my normal clothes!'

But thankfully she was joking, a mud-tinted smile appearing before Col could run away, which he was sorely tempted to do, and all the way back to his sofa and the digestive biscuits.

'But seriously why *are* you here? It's the summer holidays. Shouldn't you be off doing . . . kid things? Clash of Steel has about fifty members. You know the age of the youngest?'

She took another hit on the vape. And, as white rose from her nostrils, Col shrugged and turned to Lucy.

'Seventeen?' she asked.

'Twenty-four,' came the reply. 'But, and don't repeat this, the bloke looks like he's in his forties. Is that beard irritating you, love? You keep scratching at it. Still, we *do* need some kids!'

Col dropped his hand from his face. An awkward silence followed as the woman continued to suck at her vape. Was this a test? A strange kind of induction ceremony? Stones had given them both money, assuming there'd be a membership fee, but they'd not even had to tell anyone their names yet.

Lucy was usually so forthright. She rushed into action. Why wasn't she saying anything now? Why was she just standing there, playing with her princess hair? It was as if the costume had robbed her of her voice.

'For as long as I can remember, I always wanted to learn sword-fighting,' Col said as confidently as he could manage. 'Like, is it best to stab or to whack? That kind of thing. You know? Technique.'

He mimed swinging a sword and made a 'whoosh' sound. It was all very embarrassing.

With a speed that left them shocked, the woman returned her vape to her pouch, manoeuvred herself between them and put an arm round their shoulders.

'Okay, well, why didn't you say earlier? I'm Karen, Clash of Steel's learning coordinator. And you might be in luck, young man. Just needed a smoke, that's all!'

She nodded at the kids and, pushing them forward, shouted, 'Fresh blood!' to a passing peasant who was stalking a loose chicken.

(And her teeth really *were* like that, decided Col.)

CHAPTER
19

Karen led them along a tree-lined path, which opened on to a large lawn. There were more people here, all dressed a thousand years out of fashion, standing in groups, some sitting in deckchairs even. There were a few gazebos too. And flags, triangle pennants, attached to plastic poles that, if there'd been any wind, would have rippled in the air. Their colours, unlike those of the re-enactors' costumes, were bright. It was a little like a village fair or car-boot sale, but with more weapons and weirdos. Well, more weapons, at least.

Karen was talking about how she was only here to bag a rich knight, but Col was finding it hard to concentrate. She spoke in a long stream and was happy enough to carry on without contribution from the kids, which was fine by them because both were trying to focus on nearby peasants to see if any were Ross and/or were holding impressive swords.

That said, the huge figure made from sticks, standing centrally in the lawn and positioned over what looked like an unlit bonfire, was quite distracting. It was very tall, maybe the height of a double-decker bus.

Col tapped Lucy's arm. 'Look at that!' he hissed, and obviously Karen heard.

She smiled. 'Don't you worry about him! That's just our little wicker man.'

'Wicker what?' asked Col.

'You know the tradition of burning a guy on Bonfire Night?' she said.

Col wasn't sure that he did, but Lucy nodded, so he copied her.

'That's just our version. They're meant to be bigger, but health and safety, you know? We'll do that next weekend. After the display. Yep, there'll be a big fire soon all right.' Smiling at the kids, Karen obviously remembered something she'd forgotten to do. 'Actually, what I *am* thinking is what are your names?' she asked. 'You'll need to fill out membership cards. It's two pounds fifty, but it's worth it because you get money off sandwiches. But not ice cream, so don't get too excited.'

They continued walking. Lucy said her name, and Col said his, and Karen asked, 'Like the hurdler?' and he said yes. Lucy glared at him like *this* was a problem and not the fact that on the first occasion of being asked, they'd forgotten Stones's advice *not* to give their real names.

'Looks like you're in luck,' said Karen. Col turned to see what she was pointing at.

Let's call it a crowd. We're not talking Premier League amounts of people – more like village green and a cute dog. But there were sufficient re-enactors standing in a circle round *something* that meant it wasn't instantly obvious what that *something* was.

It was Lucy who realised first. 'Sick,' she said. 'We used to do this at school. Well, one of my schools.'

Col wondered how many schools she'd attended, but didn't think now would be a good time for that kind of conversation. Anyway, they'd already snaked through the bystanders and could see what was occurring.

A sword fight.

His first thought? Panic. It was Ross. Very obviously Ross. All chest and top-heavy with hair. Fighting a woman. Chainmail tinkled over his chest and legs, a long white 'vest' (I guess?) reaching to his thighs. Those parts of his face that weren't beard were very red.

His opponent wasn't dressed for fighting. She was in a long black gown and had the most amazingly coloured hair, red with flashes of blonde, more like the colour of fire than anything else, and the whitest of white teeth, which actually reflected the sun, no word of a lie.

She moved slowly, but easily avoided Ross's wild swings. Neither of them were holding *the* sword – Conyers' sword – in fact, neither were actually *sword* swords, both weapons being wooden and looking like they'd come from a giftshop.

'That's Dr Draco,' whispered Karen.

Unlike Lucy, Col didn't know a lot about sword-fighting. Apart from the obvious – that, umm, you were meant to poke each other with swords. But it didn't look like Draco was doing that much attacking.

Ross, grunting, would thrust forward or sweep across or chop down, but every time Draco leant back or sidestepped away. The crowd loved this, cheering at each of Ross's failed attacks. It even began to get boring.

Thankfully it wasn't much longer before Draco, like a cat tired of toying with a mouse, decided to finish her opponent.

Ross ran at her, Draco sidestepped and, as he passed, she touched his ankle with her foot. It was enough to make him lose his balance. He went tumbling down in a gust of metal, an experience you'd imagine he was getting tired of, turning over on to his back, legs scrabbling to get up again. But, with a sweep of her arm, Draco pressed the tip of her wooden sword to his throat.

'Do you concede?' she asked, with the point clearly digging into his skin. He nodded. 'Say it?'

Eyes flashing with resentment, he said, 'You tripped me!'

'*Do you concede?*' She dug the tip further into his neck.

'I concede.'

'Excellent!' called Draco, withdrawing the sword and offering a hand to help up her vanquished foe.

At this, the crowd combusted into applause. Everyone apart from Col, that was, until Lucy elbowed him in the ribs.

'Ow,' he said, clapping.

CHAPTER
20

The crowd, now seeming to contain every single person in the castle grounds, stopped clapping and stood in complete silence.

'Thanks for watching, everyone!' said Draco. 'Another great effort from our Ross. But I'm sure we've all got work to do.'

Instantly the audience began to dissipate.

A young man, head bowed, came for Draco's sword, exchanging it for a small red purse (or possibly a handbag – I'm not an expert on such accessories) that she airily hung from her shoulder.

'Doctor Draco!' said Karen. 'Well played.'

There came some grumbling from Ross, which everyone ignored.

Draco approached Karen and the kids in the manner of royalty at a walkabout outside a newly opened school or clinic for mistreated rabbits.

'Now, who do we have here? Children? How marvellous!' She smiled. It appeared a shade . . . *engineered*. As if there were a mechanism of tiny cogs and wheels beneath her skin. 'My, what a lovely beard.'

Under the fake facial hair, Col couldn't help but smile back, like when you feel forced to yawn on seeing someone else do so. It might well be, if you believed Stones, that Draco had organised the suspicious digging in Col's hometown; it could indeed be true that she'd found a sword that should be returned to its (dead) owner because otherwise the world would end. But none of this meant she couldn't also be nice. Even Col's evil uncle Sebastian had once got him a decent Christmas present. So let's give her the benefit of the doubt, shall we?

'New members, Doctor Draco. Young ones too. I escorted them from the car park!'

Karen spoke like a three-year-old who was proud to have used the potty successfully.

'*Doctor Draco?*' Draco shook her head at the children.

'The amount of times I've told them to call me Diana. How many times, Ross?'

She addressed him without turning round. He remained looming behind her shoulder, fiddling with his sword. Unbelievably the disguises seemed to be working. Somehow he'd not recognised them.

'Many times, Doctor Draco.'

'But they still don't.' She sighed. 'Anyway, children, welcome to Clash of Steel! A silly name, but it draws the crowds. I hope you've been appropriately introduced already. Karen's great. What luck, eh, Karen? Two of them as well!'

'Yes, Doctor Draco. Incredible good fortune. Thanks, Doctor Draco.'

'Karen helps with our new members. She's our . . . umm . . . *learning* coordinator. Is that the correct title?'

'I escorted them from the car park!'

'Yes, ' purred Doctor Draco. 'I believe you've told us that already. And I'm assuming, therefore, that you two darlings will be aware of the treat afforded new members, won't you?' Draco turned from Col and Lucy, feigning a look of disbelief when it became clear they didn't. 'You mean to say that they've not been told?' she asked. 'Karen, can this be true?'

There was a pause before Karen, voice cracking slightly, replied. 'And which treat is that, Doctor Draco?' she asked, adding quickly, 'Sorry, Doctor Draco.'

'Well,' said Draco, beckoning Col forward and placing an arm round his shoulders with measured grace, 'the ice cream, of course!'

CHAPTER 21

They walked from the camp (which was how Draco described the gazebos and deckchairs on the lawn) towards the castle ruins.

'Have you been here before?' she asked Col and Lucy, moving at a pace that made it an effort to keep up. It would be wrong to say she *walked*. Her dress disguised her legs, and she advanced over the grass with such velvet smoothness that Col wouldn't have been surprised if there'd been some wheels underneath the fabric. Her red handbag swung as she went. 'It's a tremendous place. Quite Gothic.' She changed tone, sounding somewhat bitter. 'Tremendous if you're interested in history, that is. The owner, Geoffrey, is almost as old as the castle. But, no, I shouldn't speak ill of him. He allows us use of the estate, and more, without charge.'

Passing through gardens of multicoloured flowers, the sort to cause parents to *ooh* and *ahh*, they headed directly towards what remained of the castle. From this angle, you might not have guessed it was ruined. Strangely the front looked pretty complete. It occurred to Col that it resembled the letter M. Two narrow towers bookended the gatehouse. They each had three windows, if that's what you could call the break in the stones, shaped as crosses, perfect, presumably, for firing arrows from. The central gatehouse, like a gaping mouth, was fringed by a fierce-looking portcullis. Ivy clung to half its face and at the top, off-centre and over the battlements, drooped a faded and tattered Union Jack. But this front section was all that remained.

'We call it a castle,' said Draco, 'but for most of its life it was a country home. Anne Boleyn spent part of her childhood here. You've heard of her, of course.' Draco drew a finger across her neck. 'Poor woman. Educated, cultured, stylish, and look where she ended up. That's marriage for you.'

'What happened to it?' asked Lucy. 'The castle, I mean.'

'The Civil War.'

'Visitors,' said Col, almost out of breath. 'You asked if we'd been here before. Why aren't there any visitors?'

He was conscious that, since leaving the sword fight, they'd not seen anyone else, almost as if they were travelling over forbidden ground. Or being led away to some lonely place.

'It's shut to the public this weekend to allow us to practise. I can't imagine how much Geoffrey's losing in ticket sales. Still, we'll put on quite the show for him next weekend, if everyone gets themselves organised. There'll be jousting. Have you ever seen a joust?'

Alas, they had not.

'They can be brutal,' said Draco. There came another strangely mechanical smile. She was obviously amused by the mental image she'd conjured.

They crossed over the moat, which was full of water, green and mucky, and passed through the gatehouse. On the other side was . . . nothing. More grass, stinging nettles, a tall hedge up ahead where you might imagine the far walls once stood, and a drop down to the far side of the moat.

'Are we ready?' asked Draco.

She turned towards the back of the left-side tower.

Here, set in its stone, was a keypad, which she typed on, and, alongside it, a wooden door studded with metal. This unlocked with a click that sounded like breaking bone. Pushing it open, Draco stepped inside. The children didn't follow.

'What's going on?' Col muttered to Lucy. He indicated the gaping door, which, in the sunlight outside, only seemed to lead into darkness. 'This doesn't look very much like an ice-cream shop.'

Lucy shrugged. It was at this point that Col noticed a carved face above the door. It was a man's. But, instead of hair, leaves grew from the top of his head and formed a thick beard. Col felt like he'd seen the image before somewhere, and this vague memory made it all the creepier.

'Old places always have weird faces. Like churches,' said Lucy. 'Anyway, what's the worst that could happen?'

'Umm . . .' replied Col. 'She could kill us? My parents would go mad if I got myself killed.'

'She won't murder us, Col. Her hair's too nice.'

A voice floated from the doorway, echoing slightly.

'Come along, children!' called Draco. 'I won't bite! You're perfectly safe.'

Col gestured for Lucy to go first. She smiled

sarcastically, and in a flash of blue dress and blonde hair, disappeared into the gloom. I'd be lying if I said Col didn't hesitate before following.

He pulled out his phone from his tracksuit bottoms. No signal. There never is at moments like this.

'Col?' called Draco from the other side. 'We're waiting.'

CHAPTER
22

With a deep sigh, Col stepped through, checking first that the door would not swing shut behind him. He found himself at the top of some steep spiral stone steps. There was an instant chill to the air. Something about the vibes made Col think there'd be no ice creams below. He placed a hand on the wall for support. The stone was cold, and he disturbed a tangle of cobwebs. Not good.

Col descended, turning down in a corkscrew, and was shortly stepping out into the space at the bottom. He was relieved to see that it was well lit . . . whatever it was. A church crypt, that's what it reminded him of – something he'd probably seen in horror films more than in real life. It had those stone pillars that spread at the tops like trees. These supported a low brick ceiling. They didn't hold his attention for long, however, because the room sparkled with gold, silver and jewels.

Riches! Beyond your wildest dreams!

Okay, so that might be overdoing it a bit. But it looked similar enough to a grand museum exhibition, or a London jeweller's, to interest a passing burglar. The lovely shiny things, you see, were in glass cases.

'Welcome to the Treasury!' announced Draco. 'It's our stockroom, really. And we're never knowingly underpriced. Do look but don't touch. Not unless you've a few thousand to spend! And the cases catch fingerprints like you wouldn't believe, and they were only cleaned this morning. It's all alarmed too. And look . . .' She pointed to the four corners. 'We've cameras! Can't be too careful these days. There's a great deal of wealth between these walls. I just need to grab something. Won't be long.' She was at the stairs before she turned. 'And didn't we speak of ice cream? I *am* forgetful. Which flavours?'

'Vanilla,' said Lucy.

You might have thought the current situation would have made Col forget ice cream.

'Mint-choc-chip, please,' he said.

Draco nodded. 'We've another subterranean space

under the right tower. Good for keeping ice cream cold. I shan't be long.'

As she disappeared up the spiral staircase, Col unhooked his beard, and I can't begin to tell you how good it felt.

'What does subterranean mean?' asked Lucy.

'I don't know,' said Col, even though he *did* because he'd once been on a school trip to Chislehurst Caves.

'What?' said Lucy. 'Why are you glaring? Turn down your beam, bro.' She dropped her voice, conscious that the cameras could well be wired for audio too. 'Let's see if there are any sick weapons.'

She winked heavily, just in case Col didn't understand to what she was referring.

'Lucy, we need to leave. This wasn't part of the plan. We were meant to stay under the radar. Not under the ground.'

Lucy raised a finger to her lips and shushed him. 'What if it's a test? What if she's watching us?'

Col shrugged. It was amazing how free his face felt.

'Why've you taken your beard off?'

'Because it was mad scratchy.'

'Itchy, you mean.'

'Whatever. Why didn't she take us to the other place

first, the place with the ice cream? What if there's something *there* she doesn't want us to see?'

Lucy thought for a few seconds, then pulled off her wig.

'Who knows? Maybe it's a pain to get into? Maybe it's not safe for kids? Maybe she forgot? Maybe there are dogs? But, now we're here, we may as well have a look around,' she said. 'Doctor Draco said that was okay. I mean, if the sword's going to be anywhere . . .'

And so they inspected the displays. There were coins; there was jewellery; there was even a chess set, the pieces carved like little Norsemen. And, just as they were ready to give up and consider running away, at the far end of the room, in a long display case that seemed to have its own lighting, was an object made of metal that sparkled like diamonds and looked very much like a sword.

They'd found Conyers' falchion.

CHAPTER
23

'I'm not surprised she's caught your attention,' said Draco. 'Beautiful, isn't she?'

There hadn't been sufficient time to speak, let alone decide what to do. The sword lay on a velvet cushion, under a glass case. Wires were connected to the case, leading off to the wall and running up into the ceiling. It was exactly as Stones had described. Not your blunt double-edged sword from the movies, but a single blade, like a long knife, curved and beautiful. The light winked from the runic inscriptions along the silver blade; the gems in the handle blinked like meteors.

I mean, *I* don't believe in any of the curse stuff, but it certainly looked magical.

Draco had appeared as if raised by hydraulics from a

hole in the ground. Neither Col nor Lucy had heard her approach.

There was the thinnest of thin silver linings to all this drama, however; a glimmer of joy in the otherwise overwhelmingly bad feels: she'd brought ice cream. But that wasn't all. Over her left arm was draped some cream-coloured fabric.

Col decided to worry about this detail after he'd eaten. He didn't want to spoil the mint-choc-chip with thoughts of imprisonment or torture, however these might have been connected to cream fabric. Were they curtains? Was she only sorting the curtains? Okay, so the room was underground and had no windows, but there were *other* rooms, *other* windows somewhere. There were always other rooms and other windows. That's life. And that's fine. Eat the ice cream. Embrace the joy of living.

'Has anyone ever told you how much better you look clean-shaven?' Draco asked Col, handing over the mint-choc-chip. 'Good to see you've taken it off, though. I was beginning to worry that you were hiding something.'

Three small tubs of ice cream: two for the kids and one for herself. Lucy was already popping off the top and using her fingernails to lever out the plastic spoon embedded underneath, but Col waited and watched. It was only sensible to see if Draco ate her own. Because there was definitely a chance the ice cream was poisoned, even though the tubs were unopened, and there was no obvious reason *why* this woman would want them dead, despite his earlier fears. True, they'd acted fairly suspiciously so far, but they'd done nothing punishable by death. And poisoning by ice cream was quite a convoluted way to get rid of someone. This was a castle: there were bound to be ancient instruments of torture lying around. Maybe in the far corner of this room, where they hadn't yet looked.

As Draco tried to open her ice cream, made more fiddly by still holding the fabric over her arm, but attempting to keep it as far away as possible from the tub, she dropped the dessert.

It hit the stone floor with a splat, the sound echoing across the space. The impact achieved what Draco had failed to do – the top jumped off and the chocolate ice cream, somewhat melted, spewed on to the ground.

'The damned thing!' shouted Draco. And by 'shouted' I really do mean 'shouted'.

Col and Lucy instinctively took a step back. Draco had pulled her fists to her chest, squeezed into tight balls. Her face had tightened as she'd roared, her mouth widening as if she were ready to bite.

Draco relaxed her hands and moved as if to take something from the red bag still strapped across her chest. She thought better of it, though, and almost as soon as the anger had arrived it was gone.

She gave a slight cough and smoothed her hair away from her forehead. (And, miraculously, all through this she'd managed to keep the fabric hanging from her left arm.) She took a deep breath, folded the cloth and placed it on a nearby display case. (No alarms sounded.) She knelt. She scooped the spilt ice cream back into the tub with its lid. Was her temper, thought Col, the reason why everyone back at the camp seemed scared of her – refused to call her anything but Dr Draco?

'I do so hate waste,' she said as if that were a fair explanation.

She placed the dented ice-cream tub on the opposite end of the display case with the fabric. Already brown drops were seeping down the tub's side. If she'd been worried about fingerprints, imagine the mess that the chocolate would make.

'Fret not,' she said. 'I'll have someone clean up. In any case, this room will be cleared for tomorrow. We need the space.' She closed her eyes. She was composing herself for something. Col turned to Lucy. She was quite happily eating her ice cream and gave him a 'what?' shrug.

'Children,' said Draco, opening her eyes, 'allow me to make a confession. I haven't brought you here *only* to show you the Treasury and feed you ice cream.'

(Col suddenly thought of a fairy tale. It might have been the one about the house made of gingerbread, although he wasn't entirely sure why.)

'Are you going to burn us in the wicker man?' asked Lucy.

'Not quite,' replied Draco, smiling like a snake.

She explained what she had in mind.

CHAPTER
24

'I suspected this might happen,' said Stones. 'There've been rumours about Draco and the dark arts.' He made a strangely high-pitched hmm-ing sound, like a monster mosquito. 'I suppose in the short term that's good, right? We don't want her castle burning down with all the bad luck. A ritual. Honestly, I'd almost like to watch it.'

'But we won't do it, will we?' asked Col. 'The ritual. So it's not really an issue?'

Ninety minutes had passed since the ice cream, and Col and Lucy were now being driven back home by Stones.

Stones's eyes flashed in the rear-view mirror. He and Lucy disagreed with Col.

'Come on!' said Col. '*Really?*'

It wasn't that Col was big into horror films – he was too scared of being scared for that, and he didn't really know much about ancient rituals either. No, it was just that he possessed Common Sense™. That was the problem with Lucy and her dad. They were too clever; they read too many books. This divorced them from the real world. They should try lying on the sofa and playing video games once in a while.

Because, promising more ice cream, Dr Draco had asked for a favour. The sword, she'd told the children, was new to the collection. And, every time there was a new piece, Clash of Steel liked to welcome it with a . . . think of it as a kind of party. Exactly how they celebrated was determined by the piece. And this sword, well, they'd never had anything like it before, and to be honest she'd spent *years* searching for it. The design, the runes, everything about the weapon suggested that the blacksmith that created it, the great warrior that owned it, well . . . the weapon was charmed, was made powerful by magic. And not only this, Draco told them, but whoever wielded the sword would also be granted great fortune. In the course of her research, she'd read of a ceremony that, if you believed in that kind of thing, linked the sword to a new owner, a bit like an adoption. Her thinking was that, after she'd done this, coupling the sword to herself, of course, she'd buy a lottery ticket. Just to see what happened. Imagine what she could do for charity! It was worth a go, surely?

The only problem was that this ritual, or ceremony – a bit like an assembly and absolutely nothing to worry about – needed two children 'pure of thought'. What a pain! And, as Col and Lucy knew, the one thing that Clash of Steel was short of, personal hygiene notwithstanding, was children.

(Col had said that he wasn't 100 per cent sure he was 'pure of thought', but had been ignored.)

You can imagine Dr Draco's amazement, therefore, when two kids turned up *the day before she'd planned to welcome the sword to the camp*!!! It was DESTINY (maybe). Or perhaps the sword *really* was lucky. There was no need to worry, she explained. All they'd have to do was wear these cream-coloured shirts (this was how she described them, but when she lifted them up they looked very long, stretching to the knees) and read something aloud that might appear to be in a different language, but she'd write it out phonetically for them. Five minutes – ten minutes max. And, if she ended up winning the Euromillions, she'd be sure to remember them.

'Look at it this way: it's not as if she's proposing to sacrifice you on an altar,' said Stones.

'Whatever. I still don't want to do it,' said Col. 'And I'm not going to. It's suss. What if she finds out we're with you? She knows our names.'

'You told her your names?' asked Stones. 'Are you out of your tiny minds?'

'That isn't the problem. It's what happens when she finds out we're after the sword that makes my tummy go all squirty,' Col said, to a giggle from Lucy. 'It's not good. Honestly, the whole thing makes me feel . . . ill.'

'A distraction is all we need,' said Stones, completely ignoring Col's objections. 'I'll wait until you're down in the chamber and, before the ceremony starts, I'll do something that causes confusion. Then we grab the sword and it's fine.'

This plan seemed dangerously vague and worryingly optimistic.

'What? What distraction?'

'Aren't we Mr Positive today?' asked Lucy.

'I don't want to get hurt,' said Col. 'What's wrong with that? A few days ago, I happened to notice some weird chalk markings on the pavement, and now look at me. *And* my ankle is still a bit sore, thank you very much. I fell out of a window, remember?'

In a move that was as close to anger as Col had seen from the man, Stones swung the car, without indicating, into a conveniently close lay-by. He yanked up the handbrake, undid his seat belt, which pinged off and hit the door, and turned to Col with a great moaning of fabric. His eyes were wild, his face flushed.

'First, there will be great floods, with the seas rising above the mountains, but then falling back so they can't be seen. When the water returns to its original position, the world's sea animals will swim to the surface and make the most mournful sounds. Next the waters will burn from east to west and, as they do, all plants and trees will fill with blood. The Earth will be split into two parts, destroying all buildings, as great earthquakes occur much like the stones were fighting each other. After this, the world's mountains and valleys will be levelled to a plain. Those few humans who've survived will come out from their hiding places, but will no longer understand each other. And the stars will fall from the sky, and the bones of the dead will rise and, as the earth burns with water, all will die.'

Col gulped.

'That's the end of the world. It's what we're dealing with if we don't return the sword to Conyers.'

Lucy put a hand on her father's shoulder. 'You're sounding a bit mad, Father.'

'I'm not mad. I'm trying to get through to your friend here.'

'Col,' Lucy said, sighing. 'These people dug up your neighbour's garden and got *you* in trouble with the police. *And* they came into *your* garden and took the sword from under *your* lawn. Which made you fall out of your window and smash your parents' conservatory, which means your pocket money will be reduced from here until eternity. Don't you want to get them back? Don't you want . . . revenge?' Her eyes shone brightly as she said the 'r' word.

The end of the world did sound pretty bad, but it was Lucy's words that actually landed.

'What if I was to pay to get your conservatory fixed?' asked Stones. 'Would you do what I ask then?'

Col cleared his throat. 'I guess?' he said.

Because what else was there to say?

CHAPTER
25

Col decided not to tell Lucy that the only reason his parents allowed him to go back to the castle on the Sunday was that his dad thought Col was in love with her, and no matter how many times Col told him through gritted teeth that it was only that they shared similar interests, he wouldn't listen.

There'd been a *very* awkward conversation over Saturday's dinner about how maybe they'd been too harsh on him and how difficult it must be growing up. They even gave him his Xbox back. And then Dad had waited until Mum left the room to ask whether Col had 'feelings' for his new friend. And, honestly – trust me on this one – it was about the most painful thing ever.

Col *did* want to save the world. Even if he didn't really

believe that's what he'd be doing. Also, regardless of what he told himself, he *did* want to see Lucy again. And surely his parents wouldn't let him spend *all* of Sunday gaming?

But none of this decided it for him. No. It was the memory of Ross digging next door, of the patronising police, patronising adults, not a single one believing him when he said there was something dodgy about the broadband engineers. It was Dad dismissing Col's suspicions about the chalk markings. And it was the nerve of Draco's henchpeople coming into *his* garden and digging up *his* lawn and taking away a sword that, you never know, Col might well have dug up himself and sold on Vinted for many thousands of pounds.

And so Sunday came, and Dad, on the doorstep, said, 'You're the young woman I've heard so much about?'

I mean, the weird intensity of his smile didn't help. The awkward factor would definitely have been reduced, though, if he hadn't been wearing a Lycra bodysuit, having been disturbed on his exercise bike, which, unfortunately, had survived Col falling through the conservatory.

'That all depends,' said Lucy, 'on who you think I am.'

(Thankfully she wasn't wearing yesterday's princess

wig. Like Col, she was in a T-shirt. She wore shorts, while he had on his favourite Adidas tracksuit bottoms.)

Dad laughed. 'Smart,' he said. 'Col said you were.'

Col, standing alongside his father, shook his head.

'I didn't,' he said. Lucy's eyebrows fell as her lips pursed. 'I've not said anything. Not that I don't think you are.'

Dad rubbed Col's hair, which was quite annoying actually, because Col had only just finished putting some reworkable pliable fibre product in it.

'Phil!' called Mum from the depths of the house, and Col had never been so pleased to hear her.

'Ah! To be young!' said Dad. 'Well . . . have fun.' Col stepped from the house. 'And don't do anything I wouldn't do!'

'What does your dad think we're up to today?' asked Lucy as they got into her dad's car, not sounding particularly happy and putting on her seat belt in a way you might interpret as overly aggressive.

Col didn't reply. And Lucy didn't push it. Thankfully.

As the car headed out of town, Col noticed an open cardboard box in the footwell next to him. Inside were six thick tubes, each about the size of a half a baguette. They looked like fat fireworks.

'What are these?' he asked.

'If you're talking about the box, they're smoke grenades,' said Stones with a lightness that suggested this wasn't a disturbing and unusual revelation. 'To distract Draco and her henchmen.'

'Hench*people*,' said Lucy.

'During the ritual,' said Stones. 'It's fine. I bought them online. They're not toxic or anything. Well . . . you're not meant to set them off in a restricted area, and I'd try not to breathe in the smoke, but I'm sure it'll be okay. Flooding the room with water would be too dangerous obviously. As would starting a fire. So I lob in a couple of these, you grab the sword in the confusion, we get back to the car and drive to the burial site and bingo: mission complete. They're banned in six countries, by the way, so they must be good.'

'Tell him the problem, Dad,' said Lucy.

'Sure, honey. There's a small issue, Col, but nothing insurmountable.'

'He *still* doesn't know where the burial site is,' said Lucy, and Col could hear the eyeroll in her voice.

'It's fine. We have time.'

'Tell him the other problem, Dad,' said Lucy.

'Well, technically we *don't* have time. I . . . umm . . .

there was a mix-up with dates. I checked Amis's diaries. The sword needs to be reunited with Conyers before midnight. Tonight.'

'Tonight?' asked Col, thinking that surely Lucy's dad was joking. 'As in *tonight* tonight? You said we had until the end of the month.'

Dr Stones turned, half smiling. 'I know, right?'

'Focus on the road, Dad!'

Col thought back to the relay race, which was just over a week past, but felt like years ago.

'I'm not good with time pressure,' said Col. 'It causes –' what was the right word? – 'anxiety.'

'It's fine, kid,' said Stones, now looking at Col through the rear-view mirror. 'We've got hours. I'll drop you two off, then carry on with my research at the church. I know the rough area of the burial site – it's somewhere nearby. And by the time Lucy texts me half an hour before the ritual's about to start, we should be fine. Don't worry. It's all under control. Really.'

CHAPTER
26

'It's so *not* under control,' said Lucy.

They stood in the castle car park. Karen, vaping, was striding towards them from the gardens.

'Things will work out,' said Col. 'But . . . you do know there's no phone signal here, right?'

'What?'

'Your dad said you were going to text him. There's no reception.'

'Why didn't you say?'

'And how are my two beauties this morning?' asked Karen, still covered in mud. 'Well rested? Full of beans?'

Karen swapped her vape for two credit-card-sized slips that she pulled from her pouch. Membership cards. She handed them to the kids, who looked at them as a dog might a Physics textbook. Eventually Col put his in his pocket.

'I had Crunchy Nut Cornflakes for breakfast,' said Lucy. 'Not beans.' She didn't give Karen any further time to engage with this response. 'And I'll need to ring my dad sometime today, but –' she turned to Col as if it were his fault – 'my colleague says there's no phone signal.'

Karen smiled. As she did, tiny cracks in the mud, like veins, ran across her cheeks.

'Phones are banned. There were no phones in the Dark Ages,' she said.

'Maybe that's why they called them the Dark Ages?' said Col, risking a joke.

'Well, no, it was Petrarch who first coined the term. He was suggesting that the post-Roman centuries were dark compared to the light of classical antiquity.' There was a delay before anyone spoke. 'But if you go up the right-hand tower, all the way to the top, there's reception there. We had to call the fire brigade a few months back when someone, I won't tell you who, got their head stuck in a twelfth-century helmet. You'd have to ask permission from Doctor Draco, of course.'

And, with the announcement that they had a ton of

jobs to complete, she turned. Col and Lucy exchanged looks, like actors with stage fright about to step out from behind the curtain, and followed.

'So . . . if you pop on the robes and have a quick look at the script, we're good to go, I think. Sorry, do you want anything to drink? More ice cream? I should have started with that. I *am* sorry. Where are my manners?'

I don't know how good your imagination is, but try this: picture a tent. Not one you'd lie in listening to the rain, but more like one in which a king might sit. Wooden chairs covered in animal skins would face this throne from across a huge and sturdy wooden table. At the entrance of the tent, two guards with pointy pikes would stand, their faces showing that they meant business.

'May I have a Coke Zero, please?' asked Col, trying to make his voice as deep as possible and holding his hand over his mouth.

Draco, seated, turned to look at Ross, who stood beside her like a scolded dog.

'Have we met before?' he asked Col. 'It's been bugging me since yesterday.'

Draco, with a strained smile, explained that Ross didn't like children.

'No,' said Ross. 'It's not that. I mean, I don't, it's true. But this one.' He pointed a sausage finger at Col. 'Without his fake beard, he looks . . . familiar.'

He eyed Col as if looking through invisible binoculars.

'Orange juice, please,' said Lucy, and Col couldn't work out whether she was trying to distract them or was genuinely thirsty.

'Ross,' said Draco, but the man continued to stare. 'Ross!' she said again, louder now, her hair seemingly growing a brighter red as her temper rose. 'These are our guests.'

'We don't have Coke Zero,' he said. 'Only regular Pepsi. And it won't be chilled.'

Col thought this might be a medieval thing before realising that he was an idiot.

'Thanks!' he said. 'That's fine.'

And, with a glower made for two, Ross left the tent.

Draco assumed the expression of someone who'd just taken a seat on an aeroplane next to a newborn baby. Col saw her red handbag on the table. There was something about the colour that unnerved him. (I mean, it was probably the fact it was blood-red, to be fair.)

'So . . .' she said, regaining her composure. 'Any

questions? It'll all soon be over, and you can get back to hitting each other with maces or whatever it is that brought you here. And then next weekend is our display and the burning of the wicker man, and people do get terribly excited about that.'

'We're doing the ritual now?' asked Lucy, face pale. 'Not this afternoon? I thought we were doing it this afternoon.'

Col dropped his hand from his face. 'I thought it'd be this afternoon,' he said.

Lucy looked at him. 'I just said that,' she said. Turning back to Draco, she continued. 'What's the rush? It's not as if the world's ending.'

If Draco reacted in any way to the possibility of the apocalypse or, more specifically, Lucy's awareness of the possibility of the apocalypse, it wasn't obvious.

'I'll be honest. The sword is only temporarily ours. A Belgian collector has offered to buy it, a very generous offer too. The sword will be shipped off tomorrow, so we need to ensure it's in the best possible state before it goes. I'd love to keep it, but –' she looked around, indicated the tent, the furniture – 'it's not inexpensive to keep Clash of Steel going. Membership fees only cover so much. And paying customers, well, they're not what they used to be. Historians like me, we need all the income we can get. And good fortune too.'

'Do you want us to pay for membership?' asked Col, forgetting everything but politeness for a second.

Draco smiled, and for once Col thought that it might have been created by actual emotion rather than clockwork.

'No, no. You're under eighteen. No fees for children! You're the next generation. You're lambs.'

'Why are you doing this ritual if you're just going to sell the sword?' asked Lucy.

Irritation flashed across Draco's face.

'You know,' she said, 'there's a story that the world will come to an end if the sword isn't returned to its original resting place.'

Both Col and Lucy did amazing impressions of having never heard this before.

'Do I believe that? Not really. But even if it does, given the state of things at the moment, it might be for the best.'

'You can't mean that,' said Col.

'You're young,' said Draco. 'You wait until you've had your heart broken.' She turned to Lucy, who dropped her eyes to the floor. 'Do I believe that this ritual of bonding will imbue me with amazing good fortune? Not really. But I've witnessed some incredible moments in my time, visions that would freeze the blood in your veins. So I ask myself, given that the sword is temporarily in my ownership, why not give the ceremony a go?' She smiled. 'Nothing ventured, nothing gained! And everyone here loves to dress up!'

A flap of canvas and heavy footsteps indicated Ross's drink-laden return.

'Your parents don't own a pub, do they?' he asked as he handed Col the Pepsi. 'The White Hart?'

'Nope,' said Col, dropping his head and not daring to look the man in the eye. 'You must be thinking of someone else. I'm always told I look like other people. It's because of my face. I've a very common face.'

By the way Ross snorted, you could tell that he wasn't convinced. At this, Draco announced that she'd be leaving to ensure the Treasury was ready for their ritual.

'Think of it like a Nativity play. I'm sure you've both been in one of those.'

Before she left, she whispered something in Ross's ear. Whatever it was she said, it made him smile.

After finishing their drinks, the kids took turns to duck behind a curtain in the corner of Draco's tent. Here they pulled on their 'robes' over their clothes, 'robes' being the word that Draco had used to describe the long cream shirts.

Given that only yesterday he'd been wearing a thick fake beard, Col didn't feel too silly.

'Time to go,' announced Ross, but before they left the tent he turned, like he'd only just remembered, and said, 'Oh yeah. One more thing. Doctor Draco's instructions. Give me your phones.'

Lucy audibly gulped. You could hear the shock in her throat.

'What?' asked Col. 'We don't have phones.' He added a laugh, which, if you'd been there, you'd agree sounded far too nervous to be convincing.

Ross held out a meaty palm. 'There's no signal anyway. And you'll get them back.'

Lucy looked at Col and Col looked at Lucy.

Ross sighed. 'It's like at concerts, you know? When they take the audience's phones away. Dr Draco doesn't want any photos of the sword ending up on social media. It might jeopardise the sale.'

'How about we promise not to take pictures but keep the phones?' said Lucy.

Ross's hand turned into a fist with the index finger

swinging back and forth: 'No.' And then he opened his fingers up into a palm.

There was no point arguing. They handed them over. Col was sure that he'd think of something. Or, failing that, Lucy would. Because they'd have to, wouldn't they? Or else they'd be to blame for the end of the world, and that would majorly suck.

CHAPTER
27

It was a nightmare.

Admittedly not the most original thought, but it was definitely the first Col had on stepping into the crypt. The shadows, the stone, the hooded figures. He willed himself awake, but it didn't work. Why? He was already awake, and this was his new reality. Also, it was proper spooky.

The display cases had been pushed back behind the darkest of dark cloth that hung like tapestries down the brick walls. Well, all the cases but one. Conyers' sword remained on display, the protective glass removed, the weapon lying on its crimson velvet. All Col needed to do was take a few steps and touch it. Its presence, its *obviousness*, though, didn't stop it from looking weirdly holographic. Was it the shimmer of the silver blade? The winking red, blue and yellow of the gemstones set in its handle? Or was it just that Col hadn't eaten a decent breakfast?

It could have been the light. The electrics were off. Instead eight thick candles sat in large metallic bowls, positioned on top of what looked to be broken stone pillars, which hadn't been there yesterday, in lines of four that ran parallel to the long sides of the sword's case at coffee-table height. The bowls amplified both the light and the candles' flickering, sending nervous shadows racing across the dark walls.

It felt like a vampire's living room. And I don't mean that in a positive way.

At the other end of the sword, facing its tip, stood Draco and Karen. Karen, like her boss, wore a hooded robe. Gone was the eccentric, mud-stained woman of earlier. Now she appeared wraithlike, threatening.

'I want to go home,' said Lucy, which was exactly what Col was thinking. 'I've reached my limit. This is too weird.'

'Don't worry,' said Draco. 'We'll soon be done. And then you can have all the ice cream you want.'

You'd have hardly noticed the flicker in the corner of

her eye, the spasm of her muscles, an algorithm inside going wrong.

'I didn't like the ice cream,' said Lucy. 'It tasted . . . strange.'

Col nodded, gulping down his fear. 'It did a bit,' he said. 'To be honest, no offence.'

Even with her hood up, Draco's hair could still be seen, those fiery strands that poked out glowing in the gloom. If Col's mum had been here, she'd definitely have asked what conditioner she used.

The sound of the door closing echoed down the stairs. With it came the failure of Stones's plan. There was no way now he'd be able to toss down a smoke grenade. And, standing in the crypt, Col wasn't entirely sure that it would have worked anyway. Presumably someone could have just picked it up and thrown it back. They don't *instantly* fill the space with smoke. The SAS don't buy their grenades from Amazon.

Ross emerged from the spiral staircase into the crypt. He waited behind Lucy and Col, standing guard at the exit, arms tightly folded across his thick chest. As they turned to look, he shrugged.

'What?' he said.

'Do you have your lines?' asked Draco. The kids

returned their focus to her and nodded. 'What will happen now is that you read them out together, following the sounds as precisely as possible, please, and then I'll cut my thumb very slightly so a drop of blood falls on the blade. Following that, it's my turn to say a quick thing. And then we're done. Understand?'

'She's *not* a robot, then,' whispered Lucy to Col.

'I'm sorry?' said Draco, seemingly offended.

'Why us?' asked Lucy. 'And why blood? I don't want to do this.'

Was she stalling? Did she think her dad was on the way? Or that Col had a plan? Probably not. On both counts.

Draco turned to inspect Karen. But Karen's head was bowed, almost as if she were praying.

'I asked earlier if you had any questions . . .' said Draco.

'In all fairness,' said Col, both deciding to help Lucy out and also suddenly feeling like he could really do with visiting the toilet, 'we didn't know about the blood before.'

Draco sighed. 'Well,' she said, speaking at double speed, 'without going into the details, a number of Anglo-Saxon or pagan ceremonies required the presence of children. We're not talking child sacrifice or anything like that – don't worry.'

She didn't smile. Neither did Col and Lucy.

'But the children represented vitality, youth, rebirth. And the same's true of this. Now I don't believe that what we're about to perform will make a blind bit of difference to anything. But we're a re-enactment society, and re-enactment's what we do. As I've already explained, if I don't end up being gifted immense good fortune, then I can live with that. But if all it takes is a little blood, why not give it a go? You don't get anywhere in this world by playing it safe. So let's continue. Children, if you will: read your parts.'

Col and Lucy raised their scripts. And slowly they began reading. What else was there to do? As they struggled over the strange sounds, Draco and Karen (who had to be nudged to be reminded to do similarly) stretched their hands out over the sword. It looked to Col ominously like they were casting a spell.

He stopped reading. His parents would go *mad* if they thought he'd got mixed up in magic. They had *very* strong opinions about Harry Potter.

'What now?' demanded Draco. 'Why've you stopped? What is this?'

'What are we reading?' Col asked. 'What do the words mean?'

Any pretence at good humour had evaporated. Draco snapped at him.

'I'll give you the translation later. Just get on with it. Start from the beginning. Never work with animals or children, they say, but I'd have been better off teaching the pigs to read.'

'Wait!' said Ross. He seemed almost surprised that he dared issue an order in the boss's presence. 'I *have* seen these two before!'

'We've established that, darling. Now –' Draco spoke from between gritted teeth – 'let's get on with it.'

'*He* was the boy that called the police. It was *his* house, *his* garden where we found the sword. And the girl! She was the one in the park with the weird chat! The one I chased. Troublemakers. They're not here for re-enactments! They're here for the sword!'

Col's insides didn't react well to Ross's sudden burst of memory. He turned to Lucy, and she turned to him. They offered each other half-smiles.

Draco, for once, had no words.

'I knew you two were dodgy,' said Karen. 'Didn't I

say? Wearing that beard and being judgemental about my vaping.'

Draco wrung her hands. 'It doesn't matter,' she said finally, although not sounding particularly convinced. 'They're here now. They can still read their parts. You can interrogate them afterwards.'

'But—' began Ross.

Draco roared in response. 'Why must everyone question my every decision? Do what you're paid to do or I'll have you clearing up after the chickens for the next century.'

Ross dropped his eyes to the floor. 'Yes, Doctor Draco,' he mumbled.

Col's gaze flicked round the room. *Think. Think. Imagine this is a game. There's always a clue in the setting. Something the designer has left for you. Those pillars. Holding the candles. Yes! If I knocked over the closest one . . .*

'Copy me,' he whispered to Lucy.

'Yes, yes,' said Draco. 'Say the same words as the boy. Now get on with it before my patience snaps.'

This time, the children read the whole piece. Draco's face shimmered with excitement, the earlier anger now buried.

'Bravo!' she said. 'Well done! See, Ross? Now hand me the ceremonial dagger, Karen!'

Karen dug a hand into her robes.

'Ready?' hissed Col to Lucy. She nodded, smiled.

And, with a kick of which Jackie Chan (Google him) would have been proud, Col struck his trainer against the closest candle pillar.

The impact did exactly as hoped, and the column tumbled. From zero degrees to forty-five, a falling tree, striking the next column with a whip-crack.

Lucy kicked out too, left arm held behind her to balance, the sole of her right foot striking. And Col could almost have hugged her! Woof – she got it exactly right. The thwack of Converse against stone made a satisfying sound.

And, either side of the sword, the pillars tumbled domino-style, their candles toppling to the ground, flickering, fading, dying. Dust rose as, rumbling, clattering and thumping, the lights winked out one by one. And, only seconds after Draco had asked for a dagger, the crypt fell into complete and absolute darkness.

CHAPTER
28

'The lights!' screamed Draco. 'Turn on the lights!'

Col's instinct was to dive for the stairs. But his foot caught against something thick, and he fell to his knees. He felt the air swirl round him, movement. There was grunting. Someone, Karen maybe, yelped. A rustling of clothes, some coughing. And there, somehow emerging from the darkness, was Draco's hair. But not just her hair. The outline of her body. Actually, more than the outline.

Fire!

Around her, the fabric hanging from the walls had caught alight, and *that* was the source of light now. As Col stood up, there was more movement, more rustling, a second maybe and then the flames doubled in size, hungrily eating up the dry and moth-bitten cloth, throwing rippling shards of light across the crypt, a whooshing roar sounding as they did so.

Ross had joined Draco and Karen at the far end of the sword, like a guard dog instinctively moving to protect its owner. Smoke, great clouds of it, billowed up round them. Soon none of them would be able to breathe. Col looked over his shoulder at the pencil outline of the beckoning exit, but something stopped him. It wasn't a thought or anything abstract like that. It was Lucy. She held on to his arm with her left hand as she reached for the sword with her right.

'No!' shouted Draco. 'Don't you dare, child! Stop her, Ross! Stop her, Karen!'

Who knows? Maybe it was Ross's huge chest that did for him. Did his enormous lungs mean he was quicker to breathe in the smoke, which now filled the room to waist-height? Whatever the reason, he didn't stop Lucy. He doubled up and started to cough.

The flames danced. It was a disco of fire. They crackled too. And the other side of the crypt caught alight now in a great woof of combustion, a sheet of heat travelling across the cramped space.

With the fire flashing against the blade, Lucy lifted the

sword from the case. Clearly it was heavy. She let go of Col to carry it with two hands. Pointing its tip towards the adults, Lucy stepped backwards. Col did too, coughing only slightly.

'I told you I wanted to go home!' called Lucy.

Draco, covering her mouth with her robe, pushed Ross forward. He stumbled past the empty case and towards the kids, hands outstretched like a zombie. He lurched forward, grabbing, but in a move familiar to the sword-fighting audience Col and Lucy avoided him by way of a simple sidestep. He staggered past, striking the back wall with a nasty crack and falling to disappear below the smoke, as if sinking underwater.

'Ow!' called Col, his hand to his cheek and feeling the warm wetness of blood.

In dodging Ross, Lucy had swung the sword. Its tip had scored a vertical line straight down from Col's right eye. And it didn't half hurt. Worse even than a nick when shaving. (You'll have to take my word for this.)

Lucy didn't apologise. Because, balancing the blade on her shoulder, she was already coughing her way up the spiral staircase. Col, his face hurting almost as much as his lungs, followed. They pushed open the door and exploded out into the smoke-free morning. Here the air was as fresh as mint but, as they filled their lungs with oxygen and relief, they didn't stop moving.

'I've an idea!' said Col, pulling at Lucy's arm, leading her to the right-hand tower.

As he'd hoped, the door to this had no keypad. And, although it had a lock, a quick pull at the handle showed that it was open. This, thought Col, was fantastically lucky.

The two children dived inside, pulling the door shut behind them, at exactly the same time as Draco, Karen and a limping, spluttering Ross emerged through the black clouds of smoke into the courtyard, looking a bit like they'd been ejected from hell.

They didn't see our heroes, though. They didn't even suspect they'd escaped into the other tower. In fairness, the three rogues didn't do anything much for a good thirty seconds, other than bend over and cough.

And, would you know it, but the tower's battlement was perfect to spy through, if, like Lucy and Col, you found yourself in the stone circle that was the rooftop. Again, it was a terrific stroke of luck that they happened to fit the lookout so well – any shorter and the angle of elevation wouldn't work; any taller and they'd be seen.

They watched Draco, Ross and Karen below, and it

took almighty self-control not to cough. Even if they had, though, it's unlikely they'd have been heard. The left tower's fire roared, smoke pumping out of its door like an overly keen dry-ice machine at a school musical. It was surely only a matter of time before the whole tower went up in flames.

'Find them!' ordered Draco, her hood down, her hair making it almost look like her head had caught fire. 'What are you waiting for?'

'Shouldn't we call the fire brigade?' asked Karen.

'What? And have them discover what we've got stored down there? No. Gather the troops with water. It's an enclosed space – with enough buckets, we'll be fine. Ross, locate the children. They won't have got far. They'll be on the grounds somewhere. *Go!*'

Karen hurried away, followed by a hobbling Ross. Draco, coughing, turned back to the tower door. Pulling her robe up over her mouth, she pulled it shut. This done, she wheeled round to inspect the area, and Col and Lucy ducked. When they dared look out again, she'd gone.

CHAPTER
29

'How bad does it look?' asked Col.

'There's still smoke coming out, but I can't see any flames.'

'Not the tower. My face.'

Lucy ducked down and sat with her back to the stone of the battlement, shuffling close enough to Col to inspect his cheek.

'It's fine. It's not even bleeding.'

Col touched the wound with his fingertip. The pain was sharp, that was for sure, but, checking his finger, it seemed she was right. There was no blood. In fact, it felt more like a burn than a cut.

'I'd better not scar,' he said.

'Or what? You'd look badass. Like a pirate.'

Lucy laughed. And, despite himself, because he very much didn't want to look like a pirate – imagine the bullying, the nicknames! – Col joined in. Quietly.

The sword stood balanced against the far battlement, its tip pointing towards the sky. They'd pulled off their robes, which were now heaped in the centre of the rooftop like a pile of washing.

'Won't you scratch its handle like that?' asked Col.

Not that it mattered, he thought, given that the plan was to bury it, which seemed a shame. It didn't look like a weapon. Stabbing was beneath it. It belonged in a gallery. Whoever had crafted it was an artist. And you'd not think the sword to be hundreds of years old either. Col wanted to touch it, wanted to own it. It was difficult to take his eyes off it.

'That's the pommel, the bit at the end,' said Lucy, pointing it out. 'And then you've got the grip. The bar that stops your fingers getting mashed is the cross guard.'

Col nodded his approval. It must be nice to know stuff.

'It looks sick, doesn't it? I mean, sick good.'

'A weapon fit for killing massive worms or whatever it was,' said Lucy.

The conversation was cut short by movement below.

The kids scrambled up to spy. At ground level, Karen led a group of a dozen or so re-enactors. Each one held a bucket, water splashing over the brim as they hurried towards the burning tower.

Was there less smoke rising from round the door? It was difficult to say, not least because there was definitely *some* escaping from cracks in the tower's stonework.

Karen approached the keypad. 'Ow!' she yelped! 'That's hot!' Wrapping her hand in her skirt, she tried again.

'Hadn't you . . .' began one of the bucket carriers.

But it was too late. Karen was already opening the door. It seemed that as soon as she touched the handle there came an explosion, a huge fireball that boomed from the doorway, an orange roar that flattened all those in the courtyard and rose into the sky, reminding Col of the mushroom shape he'd seen in documentaries about nuclear bombs.

The kids' tower rumbled as if they were living through an earthquake, and they were knocked down by the barrage of heat that came speeding from the explosion and through the stone crenellations. On the floor, they were calmed a little by the stones' coolness. And by 'a little' I mean 'not very much'.

'Never open a door in a fire,' panted Lucy, her left cheek to the ground. 'Backdraught. All that sudden oxygen makes the fire a thousand times worse.'

Fair enough, thought Col, right cheek to the ground. She *did* know a lot.

Remembering her carefully curated persona, though, Lucy added, 'We had a safety assembly last year.'

They returned to their vantage point. Col hoped that nobody was hurt. Mainly because that would be bad, but also because he'd feel the need to do something and, for the time being, he was happy being safely hidden at the top of the tower.

Thankfully the re-enactors appeared winded rather than wounded. It wasn't long before they were on their feet again, brushing themselves down. Smoke flowed from the open door, but now less densely, more candyfloss than cotton wool. Col could see no flames.

After five minutes of the re-enactors standing about and discussing whether they should go and tell Dr Draco about the explosion, a tall man who was wearing swimming goggles and a face mask (both of which looked weird, but not as weird as his peasant's tunic that appeared to have been made out of a potato sack) said he'd go in, and did anyone have a torch. A tiny woman dressed like a nun handed over her phone. At this, Lucy looked at Col. She nodded to indicate that they should drop and confer.

'Our phones,' she said. 'Ross has got our phones.'

And Col was struck by the almighty challenge he'd face on returning home. How was he going to explain to his parents why he smelt of smoke, the cut on his face, the lost phone? This was all assuming, of course, that he ever got there.

'Your dad knows where we are,' he said. 'And it's not like he's going to be angry with you. Unlike mine.'

'You don't understand,' said Lucy, her face showing the same fear Col had seen earlier. 'I'm not worried about getting told off. Partly because I'm not eight. But mainly because of my backdrop. That's the klaxon-sounding problem. It's a picture of me and Dad. All Ross or Draco or whoever need do is wake the phone, touch the screen and they'll see us both together.'

'So? Ross has already worked out we're after the sword.'

(Col's backdrop, for no justification other than he found it funny, was a dog smoking a pipe.)

Lucy rolled her eyes. 'She knows my dad, Col. They worked together. She'd be able to trace him. She'll understand *why* we're after it.'

'Right,' said Col, turning and pulling himself back up to the battlement.

'What do you mean "right"?'

'I mean . . . we'll think of something,' he said. 'Don't worry. Chill.'

'Don't tell me to chill,' said Lucy. 'It's the kind of thing babysitters say.' Col didn't reply. Instead he touched his cheek and flinched. 'And I see what you're doing. Don't try and guilt-trip me either.'

But here they stopped talking because, down below, the tall man in goggles and mask had returned.

'The fire's out,' he said. 'Visibility's bad and it's a job to breathe, but the cases look like they've protected most of the stock.'

'Doctor Draco will be pleased!' said the tiny nun, bouncing.

'Yes,' announced Karen, who up until now had been noticeably quiet. Still, it hadn't been *that* long since a massive firebomb had knocked her on to her backside.

'How about we—' began the tall man, his mask pulled down and his goggles pulled up.

'Let me think!' Karen spoke over him in a Draco-like outburst, a miniature explosion herself. 'My bum doesn't half ache.'

They waited as she scratched her chin as if only pretending to think. Eventually she came out with a plan.

'Harvey. You're in charge of recovering the objects. We'll form a line up the staircase. Put the stock in the buckets, and we'll pass it out that way. Okay?'

The gang nodded in agreement, but otherwise movement was lacking.

'Let's get busy, then!' said Karen, clapping her hands together. 'Like busy bees! But be careful! You know what'll happen if you drop a candlestick or dent a gold cup. You'll be flayed alive!'

And as she laughed at this idea, and made some buzzing noises, Lucy and Col dropped down again.

'What now?' he asked.

'We wait,' said Lucy. 'We wait.'

CHAPTER 30

I don't think Col really *had* fallen asleep. When you're sitting on top of a castle, and angry, violent people are after you because you've got a sword that, unless soon buried, might destroy the world, and also your cheek hurts and you've lost your phone, and the stone wall you're leaning against is really uncomfortable, and the sun keeps blasting down its insistent heat, well . . . it's difficult to nod off. Especially if the person you're with keeps asking whether the re-enactors have gone when she could quite easily check herself.

But . . . he *had* drifted into that state where thoughts are a breeze away from floating off, and your eyelids, if not closed, are particularly heavy.

And so the sudden loud voice coming from below,

accompanied by Lucy shaking his arm, didn't only shock Col into full consciousness, but actually caused him pain, a tight knotting of his internal organs, parts of his body which, you have to admit, had suffered quite substantially so far in this story.

'Look!' hissed Lucy, already returned to the nearest battlement.

Col joined her and, as you'd probably expect, looked specifically at the woman whose voice had made him jump in the first place. She was not in costume. Unless, of course, she was only *pretending* to be a police officer. She wasn't the only new arrival either – there was another police officer too, and one with a chest almost as big as Ross's. A step behind the two officers, arms folded and looking wonderfully grumpy, was a line of three firefighters.

'I'll ask again. What's going on?'

The human chain had paused. The peasant in the doorway leant against it, soot-stained, tired. The next one along scratched her head and put down a bucket. And the last was Karen, who stood alongside a collection of buckets. And, although Col and Lucy could only see the back of her head, it was pretty obvious that she was *not* smiling.

One of the firefighters stepped over to the buckets. She bent down and pulled out a gold necklace. It shimmered like water in the sun.

'Check this out,' she said. 'It's hot an' all.'

The other firefighters joined her. They too pulled out wonderful shiny objects. Apart from one. Who pulled out a bone. And yelped. And dropped it back into the bucket.

'Sorry,' said the firefighter. 'Not a fan of dead things.'

'Who's in charge here?' asked the police officer.

Karen said nothing. The police officer removed the handcuffs from her belt. They shone almost as prettily as the gold necklace. Karen decided to speak.

'That would be Doctor Draco,' she said. 'I'll take you to her.'

The police officer nodded. 'Good. And you'd better bring your –' she looked at the other re-enactors – 'gang with you too.'

'But don't you see?' asked Lucy, smiling. 'The police turning up *was* amazingly lucky. Just like finding the door down there unlocked. It's *you*, Col. Me scratching your face must have done it. Like Doctor Draco said. That's what she was trying to get from the ritual. Great fortune meaning . . . *luck*. Remember what she said about the lottery? You should buy a ticket.'

'I'm not old enough,' muttered Col, who was, it has to be said, feeling more headachey than lucky. 'And it's a cut, not a scratch.'

Lucy stood leaning against the battlement, staring out at the horizon. Col remained sitting. They'd agreed to give it twenty minutes, and if they saw nobody in that time they'd run. Where to, they hadn't decided. Col had set a twenty-minute timer on his fitness watch. He thought he'd check his heart-rate history when he got home. If he ever did.

And anyway he wasn't convinced by Lucy's reasoning. The way he saw it was that, even in the countryside, a huge explosion was likely to get *someone's* attention. It wasn't luck. Even if the police hadn't been passing, some farmer somewhere would have seen the smoke. But he wasn't able to explain all this because Lucy began saying, 'Oh my God!' and, 'I can't believe it!' and Col stood up and saw what caused these outbursts (plus, she was pointing too).

'It's Dad!' she said.

And it was. He moved unsteadily over the fields behind the castle, a strange figure darting between hay bales.

Even though he was a fair distance away, there was something undeniably Stones-y about his movements. And, of course, there was the hat. Without checking with Col, Lucy grabbed the sword, balancing its blade over her shoulder, and made to leave.

Col followed her, hoping that she didn't trip as she skipped down the steps. That would be messy. Lucy had obviously come to the same conclusion by the time she'd reached the bottom. She waited at the door, out of breath, holding out the sword in her arms, almost as if it were a child she'd been carrying.

'Can you have it for a while?' she asked. 'It's mad heavy.'

Weirdly Col didn't think it too bad. He had to hold it with two hands, but, as he hurried past the courtyard and into the stinging-nettle meadow beyond, it wasn't as if his arms ached with the weight. And, yes, I'd be lying if I said that when Col ran he didn't imagine himself an ancient warrior rushing at his massed enemies.

This would be as close as he would ever come to thinking re-enactments could be enjoyable.

They crossed the moat over a bridge (a plank of wood) and soon, as with all countryside walks, they reached a hedge. It was waist-height and had grown round a similarly sized old metal fence. By this point, Stones had seen the kids. He waved as he jogged towards their position, stumbling only slightly over the uneven ground. Lucy was waving too, but it wasn't immediately obvious to Col how they'd breach the hedge.

'Use the sword!' said Lucy. 'What are you waiting for?'

CHAPTER 31

But the hedge was thick, and the sword was valuable.

'I don't want to scratch it,' said Col.

'*I* don't want to get tortured by Draco,' said Lucy.

He raised the sword over his head and brought it down in a chopping motion, a bit like you might do if you wanted to slice a thick rope, if that's something you can picture because I'm not sure how often kids need to slice thick rope these days, more's the pity. The blade slashed through the brambles and twigs and struck the ground with a thump that vibrated up Col's arms.

And then something strange happened. The greenery that the sword had passed through wilted either side of the break, browning as it shrank back. As this happened, a clear gap in the hedge was revealed, wide enough to walk through, and one that Col had in no way noticed a second ago.

'Weird,' he said.

'Not weird. *Lucky*. What did I say?'

Okay, so the blade was still a little warm from the fire, Col thought. That's what had happened to the hedge. And a cut-through to the fields wasn't *that* freaky. People would have walked this way in the past. Or it was an ancient sheep trail or—

There was no time to discuss any of this, though, because Lucy was already through the hedge and in Stones's arms, and he was kissing the top of her head. If this had been a film, there wouldn't have been a dry eye in the audience. Her father was so excited that the brim of his hat pushed against Lucy's head and popped off. He looked over at Col, beaming but sweating too. (His face was stop-sign red.) And he panted as he spoke, releasing Lucy from his hug, stooping to pick up his hat.

'I never heard from you, and your phones went straight to voicemail, and I was deeply worried, and so I jumped in the car, and is that smoke?' But he wasn't really interested in the tower because he was gasping at the sword and holding out his hands to relieve Col of it.

As Col passed it over, Stones sagged, the weight pulling at his shoulders. 'Heavy, isn't it? But beautiful. Look!' He just about managed to keep the thing balanced while holding it with one hand. With his free hand, he pointed at the markings lightly carved into the blade. 'Runes. It's an enchanted falchion, you see. This is a spell.'

He lowered the sword so that its point rested against the field's powdery soil.

'Dad. Col got cut by it, and I think he's become, like, magically lucky.' Lucy's voice dropped. 'I can't believe I just said that. This summer has been majorly strange.'

Col angled his chin to show off his battle wound. Stones sucked air through his teeth.

'Ouch,' he said. 'Are you okay? Do you want a plaster? I don't know why I'm asking that. I don't have any.'

Col just nodded. This, he thought, was the behaviour of a true hero, especially considering who'd inflicted his wound and how he'd said nothing.

'Explaining all this to your parents is going to be a pain in the . . .' Stones's train of thought faded as he turned the sword in the sunlight, the blade winking, the gemstones sparkling. 'But look at it. Amazing. The stones shimmering as if they were cut yesterday. Can you see, Lucy? Col? Flawless. These alone are priceless.'

Col cleared his throat. 'But we're definitely *not* going to sell it?' he asked.

The Stones family turned their focus from the sword to Col. Both father and daughter looked unimpressed. Col gulped only slightly.

'Okay. I get it. End of the world. Dogs and cats living together. Mass hysteria. Fine. But if Mum ever finds out that a priceless relic was dug out of her garden, and she got no money for it, she's going to blow a gasket.'

(He didn't know *exactly* what this meant, but Mum would often warn Dad, when she was on the verge of losing her temper, that it was about to happen.)

'The car's in the car park,' said Stones eventually. 'See those trees over there? We can loop round and avoid the castle grounds and get to it that way.'

They set off. Hopefully the worst was now behind them. Literally *and* metaphorically. And amazingly too because, yes, they had been *quite* lucky, stolen phones aside. The plan *had* worked – they'd got the sword – so the next stage should be easy, right?

'Where's the burial site, Dad?' asked Lucy, possibly thinking the same as Col as Stones stumbled forward, holding the sword like you might a tree branch made of silver.

Stones cleared his throat. 'Yes, well, umm . . . it's been a busy day. And I *am* definitely closer to pinpointing the location.'

Lucy stopped. Col copied her. Stones continued walking.

'You mean to say you *still* don't know where it is? We've done our part here. I don't know if you've noticed the slicey silvery thing you're currently holding.'

'It's fine,' he said over his shoulder. 'Chill.'

Lucy flapped her arms against her sides. 'Why are people always telling me to chill?' she said.

Maybe, thought Col, it was because she needed to.

'We've got until midnight, Luce! But that doesn't mean we can afford to waste time chatting in the middle of strange fields! Come on!'

Lucy rolled her eyes and followed her dad. As Col set off, he considered how much he was looking forward to next week and, in particular, staying in bed every day.

CHAPTER 32

Ross appeared as if he had respawned. First, he wasn't there. And then, in a heartbeat, he most definitely was.

They'd reached the car park without any trouble, other than the stinging nettles that Col soon sent back to Stinging Nettle Hell with a quick flash of Conyers' sword. Stones was pulling the car keys from his linen trousers and muttering about how the answer was to be found in the church, and how maybe the kids, with their young eyes, might notice something he'd missed. And it was exactly at this point that Ross appeared.

He loomed from the other side of Stones's battered green Honda, towering over it like he'd grown since they'd last seen him.

'You!' Ross roared and, instead of rushing round the

car, he jumped on to its bonnet. The metal creaked in protest as the car's front end sank. Ross balanced like a surfer.

'Hey,' said Stones. 'I've had that car for years.'

By the time the Viking was leaping down to their side, Stones had raised his hands like a boxer, shooing the kids behind him.

'No, Dad!' said Lucy.

'It's okay,' he said. 'I boxed at university.'

Ross seemed to find this funny. A genuine smile crept across his hairy chops. It didn't last long, though, fading as he raised his fists to mirror Stones.

'You wanna fight, old man? We'll fight. I'll knock you to Folkestone and back.'

As Lucy and Col backed further off, almost without thinking, the two men shimmied this way and that, their shoes crunching against the gravel. As they did so, Col felt incredibly self-conscious about holding a sword but, no matter how much of a bad guy Ross obviously was, it wasn't like Col was going to swing a blade at him.

Not yet anyway.

And who knew what would happen? Maybe Stones *was* a champion fighter. It's not the dog in the fight, it's the fight in the dog. Or something like that? The point is it's not always the biggest dog that wins. Not *always*.

Stones got the first punch in. And, to be honest, it looked a decent hit. Lucy made an 'ooh' sound. Col said, 'Yes!' and waved the sword a bit. But, and I'm sorry to have to report this, the thump had zero effect on Ross.

The huge man looked down at his chest, where the fist had landed, as if noticing a butterfly flutter against his pecs. Then he raised his head to Stones, who continued his funny little dance, this way and that, with fists raised.

Ross pulled back his right arm and let it go. A wrecking ball against Dr Stones's chin, it thundered like a cricket ball hit for six. The Panama hat, once again, flew off. And, for a second, the doctor wavered on his heels, arms now windmilling in an attempt to keep his balance. But it was no good. He went down, slap on to his backside, on the car park gravel.

'Oof,' he said, dust rising round him.

'Now,' said Ross, turning to the kids, 'give back what you've stolen, and I might let you off.' He stepped towards them. 'Who am I kidding?' he snarled. 'I've hated children ever since I was one. You're both mincemeat.'

Lucy and Col darted round the far side of the car. Ross, sighing, lumbered after them. Lucy sprinted full circle to return to her dad, checking on him as he shakily used the wheel arch to pull himself up. She handed him his hat as if it might restore his energy.

Let's turn to Col. Because he *didn't* continue running. He held his ground. But that wasn't the only thing he held. He also held the sword out, daring Ross to go for him. Because if the man ran *into* the blade that wouldn't technically be Col's fault, Your Honour.

Ross took two steps forward, but didn't show an immediate inclination to turn himself into a human kebab. Col thrust out the sword a bit more and nodded as if he meant business. But, like a bear pawing at a squirrel, Ross swatted the weapon aside. It flew from Col's grip and hit the ground with a worrying clang.

'Hey,' said Stones over the car's roof, rubbing his jaw. 'That's a valuable historical artefact!' And, just as Col was wondering if Lucy's dad was more interested in the sword's safety than his, he added, 'And the boy's worth something too!'

Col saw this as an opportunity to run, which he took, joining the other two behind the Honda.

'I've got a plan,' he said. 'Get in the car.'

'We're not leaving you, kid,' said Stones. 'Or the sword.'

'I know. You won't. Trust me.'

At this, Ross turned the corner and faced the three of them. But instead of skipping round the other side or jumping into the car, Col did something that all the sinews in his body strained against.

He ran *at* Ross, and as fast as possible.

CHAPTER 33

Collisions are often compared to hitting a brick wall, so much so that the simile has become a cliché. I'm told that good writing seeks to avoid clichés, but (and here's the thing) running into Ross really *was* like hitting a brick wall . . . if the bricks were reinforced with steel and also surrounded by some kind of force field made of diamonds and even more bricks.

Col didn't bounce off Ross's chest, he stopped dead, and before he could regret not thinking through his plan Ross grabbed his collar and used it to lift all of Col off the ground.

'Ha!' Ross laughed as Col's feet pedalled in cartoon desperation. 'You've spirit, boy. Let me punch that out of you.'

And, as Col heard the car doors close, he managed to rotate sufficiently in Ross's enormous fist to do a fairly impressive mid-air kick, exactly where nobody wants to be kicked, mid-air or not. Yes, his foot connected with Ross's privates like a clapper to a bell, and the shock, if not the pain, was enough for the big man to drop him.

Col was running as soon as he hit the ground, sprinting towards the fire engine that was parked with its side facing the fight. As he reached it, he turned. He didn't fiddle with the hose or try to open one of the metallic compartments. He just waited.

The Viking remained standing by the car, but he'd forgotten about the occupants, who now pulled worried expressions through the windows. All thoughts of recovering the sword were also temporarily erased. With his hands cupped over his privates, he focused his entire spirit on the young boy, on his attacker, who stood, for whatever reason, in front of a fire engine.

'I knew you were trouble the first time I saw you,' he snarled. 'You and your girlfriend.'

'She's not my girlfriend,' said Col, between gritted teeth. 'We share similar interests.'

Ross was the bull. Col was the matador. And Col couldn't help but push back into the sharp contours of the fire engine. And, as he felt the pain along his spine, he wondered whether he was making a terrible mistake. It *was* an Xbox tactic, though, and this knowledge gave him confidence.

Identify a weakness in your enemy and exploit it!

Ross launched himself forward. He was still no sprinter, however, and Col's parents would have been unimpressed by the amount of time it took to cover even *half* the distance separating him from Col. Part of the issue was how top-heavy he was, like one of those characters from a flipbook in which toddlers have fun adding the top of a rhino to the bottom of a mouse. And so it wasn't as if Col had to time his dive to the split second.

Wait . . .

Wait . . .

Now!

He threw himself to his left, turning as he did to witness his plan's effectiveness, praying that he *really* was lucky.

If Ross had collided with Lucy's dad's Honda, he might have turned it over. As it was, the fire engine was much heavier, sturdier. With a noise halfway between the breaking of bones and the crushing of metal, the hulking man smashed into the vehicle and collapsed on to the ground in a pile of unmoving muscle and hair.

Now up on his feet, Col studied him briefly. As he did so, the world held its breath. Even the constant *woo-woo-wooo* of the pigeons paused. Clearly Col should be rushing to the car to make his escape, but he'd had recent experience of hitting his head and, you know, it wouldn't be cool if Ross were dead.

There came movement, though, both from the collapsed Viking – a brief stirring of the legs – and from the car. Lucy had the passenger door open and was calling.

'People are coming!' she said.

Ross's eyes flickered open, and this was enough for Col. The Honda's engine coughed to a start. Col skipped to the rear door and yanked it open, even as Stones had begun driving off. Col bundled in, sorted himself out and slammed the door.

The car bumped out of the car park and motored away along the narrow lane, engine growling. Col craned his neck to look out of the rear windscreen. A group spilt into the car park, a group including people in uniforms. Ross would be looked after or arrested. Col only hoped that the police hadn't noticed the Honda's licence plate.

'The sword!' he exclaimed. 'We left the sword!'

From the front passenger seat, Lucy lifted its hilt. She had the weapon between her legs.

'It's fine, fighter,' she said. 'Nice plan, by the way.' For once, she wasn't being sarcastic. 'Are you okay, Dad? You were punched to the ground.'

'Fine. Fine. I had my feet all wrong, that was the problem. And they used to call me Iron Jaw at university, so it's nothing I'm not used to. Maybe even knocked a little sense into me. Hmm.'

They'd reached the junction with the main road, and Col caught Dr Stones's eye in the rear-view mirror.

'We're not in trouble, are we?' he asked.

Col could just about imagine a future where he was able to persuade his parents that a lost phone and a cut cheek weren't the end of the world. It might be more difficult if the police came a-knocking a second time.

'Think about it this way,' said Stones, steering the car on to the road to Westerham. 'We're stealing back something that's already been stolen. The two cancel each other out.'

'Absolutely,' said Lucy, turning to Col with a mountainous display of sass. 'It's just a shame we don't yet know where to return it.'

'We'll need to go to my house first, Doctor Stones,' said Col. 'I've some almighty explaining to do.'

CHAPTER 34

The first sign that something was up was all the cars stopping at the side of the road. And, when they turned to look, Lucy and Col saw . . . a fire engine.

Stones began indicating left, mirroring the traffic in front and behind that was pulling over, until, that is, Lucy knocked his hand away and shouted, 'What are you doing?'

Because it wasn't just *any* fire engine. Or, more precisely, it wasn't just *any* fire-engine driver. It was Ross. And he became more obviously Ross the closer and closer the fire engine sped.

'Go faster!' said Lucy, flapping her hands to indicate the open road that lay ahead, cleared by all the drivers who'd thought this to be a genuine emergency.

Stones changed up a gear. 'I'm trying, I'm trying,' he muttered as the little Honda's engine didn't so much roar as meowed.

Col's focus was fixed through the rear window, and it was then that he realised that the screaming sound he could hear didn't come from the fire engine, and neither did the lightning strikes of blue lights. There was a police car *behind* Ross. However he'd managed to escape the officers, he hadn't succeeded in losing them.

'Dad!' said Lucy, but there wasn't much that the man could do. The speedometer trembled from 60 to 70 mph, but did so as if fighting against gravity, as if weighed down with stones (which, when you think about it, it was).

And the fire engine *really* was right behind them now, and Col could very clearly see Ross's face. It was as red as the vehicle's paint. He gripped the huge steering wheel with such anger that Col wouldn't have been surprised to see him pull the thing off and hurl it through the rectangular windscreen like a deadly frisbee. Instead, teeth bared like a wolf, he continued urging the fire engine ever closer to the Honda's back bumper.

'He's going to hit us!' said Col.

And, almost as soon as the words had left his mouth,

the cliff face of the red cab nudged against the car. Stones made a sound that wasn't particularly reassuring, his steering wheel shaking this way and that under his hands.

Cars to the left sounded their horns, thinking the Honda was refusing to pull over for an emergency.

'You're not going to outrun him,' said Lucy.

Stones turned with a look he might have borrowed from his daughter: full sass.

'You don't think?' he said.

And once again the fire engine bumped against the Honda, and once again the little car shook as if it were a ship riding a wave in a violent sea.

'No!' said Lucy as Col let out a little scream.

Ross was smiling now, enjoying himself. Col waved desperate hands. He could understand both why the Viking was determined to catch them – there were a few reasons – and how knocking the car off the road might be fun, but surely *killing* the three of them wasn't worth it?

Yet it was difficult to communicate all this through waving hands and, anyway, he wasn't even sure that Ross could see. He gave no indication of noticing Col – all Col could make out was that mad, manic grin, knuckles tight white on top of the black wheel.

Thwack! A deep bass grumble, an ominous sound. Another strike.

This time they lurched towards the central reservation and its silver crash barrier but, somehow, and with a great screaming of tyres, Stones managed to recover and keep the bonnet aimed forward, the car twitching like a fish on a line.

'Look!' Lucy pointed as the panicked cars ahead continued to peel off into the left-hand lane.

There was a sign, a junction. A town, a pub. Col didn't fully understand what she meant. I mean, he *was* hungry, but surely she couldn't be wanting to visit The Kentish Hare now? Fortunately Stones got it.

'Hold on to your hats,' he said.

And, at the moment it looked as if the junction had passed, Stones swung the car left. It nipped through the gap between a Tesla and a Land Rover. Col was too busy being catapulted round the rear seats, but if he'd been able to see Ross's face, he might have glimpsed a look of horror. Ross had swung to the left too, perhaps forgetting that he was in a fire engine and not a Honda. Fire engines, you see, are not designed for making sharp turns at high speed.

Col recovered in time to pull himself up from the back seat to watch from the rear windscreen as the fire engine, almost as instantly as the steering wheel was turned, leant over on two wheels. Had Ross been a stunt driver, he might have been able to hold this position and right the huge mass of metal.

But he wasn't. And there was also a Land Rover in the way.

Wow.

The fire engine smashed into the Land Rover with a huge shower of breaking metal, the speeding police car coming to a stop not just immediately behind it, but immediately into it, the siren fading like a dying record player. The Land Rover spun, only stopping as the fire engine finally toppled on to its side, somewhat like a dying elephant, crushing the army-green bonnet with a terrific crumple. The Land Rover driver, a man in a flat cap and Barbour jacket, did not look happy.

Stones had slowed to a trundle, but Lucy, with wild hand movements, urged him to get going.

'What are you waiting for?'

And the last image Col saw was the fire engine's door flopping open like a submarine hatch and Ross emerging, straight into the arms of two police officers.

'I've always loved this car,' said Stones fondly. 'They don't make them like this any more.'

CHAPTER 35

You don't want me describing what happened next. Honestly, you don't. If your mum's ever forced a friend's parent in for tea, you've lived it already. In summary, the Coleridges ended up sitting round the table with the Stones family, while Dr Stones politely explained why a sleepover was a great idea. Col's mum and dad, especially Mum, didn't buy it. Not until Col told the truth.

'What a wonderful imagination!' said Mum after he'd finished explaining how the world would end unless they returned this magical sword to the burial site of its warrior owner, which was nearby, but they were unsure where.

'Very creative!' said Dad, nodding.

It was agreed that Dr Stones would help Col and Lucy

work on their writing, and Col *could*, therefore, spend the night there.

Tea was finished. Hands were shaken. Col promised to be well behaved.

St Mary's Church wasn't far. First, they dropped the car off, and Stones popped inside his house, with the sword, to pick up 'notes'. While the kids waited on the pavement, ignoring the fading chalk markings, Lucy asked Col how he saw the day ending.

'Well,' said Col, 'I'd be surprised if it was, like, normal and uneventful.'

Lucy laughed, and I'd be wrong not to tell you that it made Col feel a warm kind of happy.

Stones soon emerged from the front door with a bag over his shoulder, which he explained was meant to hold golf clubs.

'But the sword fits – look! A perfect size. You just need to be a bit careful with the pointy bit at the top! I've put a football sock over it! And the golf bag has pockets for my notes and everything.' Noticing Lucy's expression, he added, 'It works. Let's not obsess over it.'

The briefest inspection would reveal that there was something deeply suspicious about the bag, but hopefully they'd not bump into any curious golfers. And anyway Col had decided not to worry. About anything. He'd let what remained of the day guide him like a stream does a stick. He'd tried telling his parents the truth, and they'd thought he was inventing some mad story.

'Do you play golf?' asked Col as they set off for the church, looking to all the world like an eccentric family heading for the putting green.

Lucy scoffed.

'I found the bag in a cupboard when we moved in,' said Stones. 'Don't worry. I'm not about to get sporty on you. For one thing, we need to save our energy. There'll be digging before the night is out.'

The church sat at the town's highest point. And so, after walking along a few roads with houses that probably contained kids having normal Sundays, maybe even complaining about how *boring* it was, something Col would *never* again do, they pushed through an ancient metal gate that creaked like an anxious goat and started on a steep path that snaked its way through a graveyard.

Some stones were broken; some had names worn away by time's unrelenting rub. Others were troublingly new. But for Col this was a well-walked short cut to the town centre and, in particular, a coffee shop that sold the *best* hot chocolate. And usually not even the creeping sense of his own mortality put him off that.

But today wasn't usual. Not by any standard.

A faded sign outside the church welcomed visitors. And the large, ancient wooden doors gaped open. Stones didn't wait, didn't speak, before taking off his hat and disappearing inside. Lucy gave Col a strained grin as they followed.

As far as these places went (churches), it was attractive enough. I mean, they all look pretty similar, don't they? You had the lines of wooden pews, which, presumably, were designed to be uncomfortable in order to stop people falling asleep. And there was much stone and many names carved into the much stone, of long-dead people rich enough to get a mention *inside*. And there were the stained-glass windows. These *were* cool because the sun was at a perfect height to shine through the various pretty shades, sending coloured reflections rippling across the chilly space.

It wasn't only Col who thought this. Having carefully deposited the golf bag in a nearby pew, hat resting on top of the football sock on top of the sword, Stones stood in the aisle closest to the entrance and swept his arms around, indicating the yellows, greens, blues.

'Amis, the man whose house burned down, the man

who first bought the sword, he gifted the church these windows. And look there! Recognise anything?'

Stones pointed at the far end of the church, past the altar. Here the windows were the most glorious of all. The bottom was a series of five narrow panels. Above these were two rows of six smaller windows. Lit from behind, it was clear to see what they represented – the usual biblical mixture of important-looking men wearing crowns and sad-seeming women holding babies, and lambs and stars and everything else in a kaleidoscope of colour. But in the central pane, the window where you'd probably expect to see Jesus, was . . . a sword. And not just any sword. It was a falchion. Even from a distance, you could make out the exact pattern of jewels in its hilt, the slight curve of the cross guard. It was *so* Conyers' sword.

'Sick,' said Lucy. 'What does it mean?'

'That's what we're here to find out.'

Stones spoke as if his words were a call to action. And seemingly without any anxiety about there only being, you know, about eight hours during which they not only had to 'find out' but also save the world.

Nobody moved.

'How long were you here today, Dad?'

Stones glanced at Col for support. But, sadly for the man, Col was 100 per cent Team Lucy.

'There was a service on this morning. Which I sat through, but couldn't really do much else. Afterwards, I searched below the window. *What if the sword's pointing at the burial spot?* I thought. It won't be the first time a church was built on a site of earlier significance. But it's thick flagstones down there. I thought about getting a crowbar in, but then I started to worry about you two, and I tried ringing, and you know what happened next.'

Lucy folded her arms in a tight knot. 'So it's our fault you've not discovered where we need to bury the sword? It's *our* fault?'

'No, Lucy. I'm not saying that. All I'm saying is . . .' His voice trailed off. 'Look, I'm not sure what I'm saying but, you know, now's not the time to be all teenage about it—'

There came the sound of movement, and all three turned. Col's throat tightened. He'd endured enough action for the day, for his life. Surely this couldn't be Ross again? And what about Dr Draco? I mean, they'd all silently assumed she'd been arrested, but you don't normally have the lead villain disappear without some kind of action-packed set piece.

A door creaked open and there was . . .

CHAPTER 36

. . . a sound like the flush of a toilet. You'd think this was the wrong order: first, the door and then the flush. But it wasn't. Because the Lord moves in mysterious ways.

A rosy-cheeked woman, with hair like a pan scourer, stepped into view. She wore a black shirt, black trousers, a white collar. And . . . a neon pink cardigan.

'The vicar!' hissed Col, although, having spent the last two days at a re-enactment, he wondered whether it might just be a costume.

'What makes you say that?' asked Lucy.

Stones turned up his charm and headed down the aisle towards the newcomer, footsteps resounding.

'Fabulous church you have here, vicar,' he said, holding out his hand. 'The windows are something else.'

The vicar shook Stones's hand, but didn't look particularly pleased to be doing so. As Lucy and Col joined the adults, Col thought he could smell flowers. Overripe, rotting even. Or maybe it was air freshener?

'Call me Rosie,' she said, sighing. 'The stained glass was a gift from a wealthy parishioner. Back when wealthy parishioners made gifts. Sir Peregrine Amis. He had a huge house in Westerham, but it burned down. You don't happen to be a wealthy parishioner, do you? Did I see you at the morning service?'

'Sorry. I'm a lecturer. And, yes, some wonderful words about temptation, I thought.'

'Pity,' said Rosie. 'We could do with a wealthy parishioner.'

'Yes,' said Stones. 'Quite. Anyway, we were interested in the stained-glass sword in particular. Such a striking image.'

Rosie laughed. Stones scratched at the back of his head. The hat had flattened his hair in a way that might have been funny if the end of the world hadn't been approaching.

'The Bible is full of swords. We can see it as a symbol of God's judgement. And, of course, you've got the symbol of the cross there too. There's something else, though, hidden in each one of the windows.' Rosie was warming up, the frostiness of having been caught in the toilet now turning to excitement at having an audience. 'Have you noticed, children?'

Compelled by politeness, the three turned, taking in the windows again. In truth, none of them saw anything that obviously stood out. The stained glass looked exactly how you'd imagine stained glass to look.

'Nope,' said Stones.

'Is it the colours?' asked Lucy.

Rosie shook her head.

And then, miraculously, Col saw. Hidden in the corner of the largest pane in each window was a letter. Each was disguised as something else – a tree, a shepherd, etc. etc. – but, once you'd seen them, there was no denying their presence. Like teachers in the supermarket.

'I know!' he said a little too loudly because he was actually quite excited. 'There are letters.'

'Very good,' purred the vicar. 'And what do they spell?'

'I can't see anything,' mumbled Stones. 'Do you have to go cross-eyed or something?'

Col turned from one window to the next, calling out the letters he saw.

'O . . . T . . . E . . .'

'What's going on?' asked Lucy, exchanging confused looks with her father. 'What's he looking at?'

'W . . . and R,' finished Col, looking to Rosie for confirmation like the class genius who knows they've got the answers correct.

'Excellent!' said the vicar. 'And what does that spell?'

'Otewr,' said Col. 'Otwre. What does Otewr mean? Is it a name?'

(In truth, this was a bit of an anticlimax. But stay with it.)

'Could be a name,' agreed Stones. 'Anglo-Saxon?'

'Tower!' said Lucy. 'It spells tower! Have you never heard of anagrams?'

Stones darted out a hand to grab a pew. The shock of discovering what was clearly an important clue almost made him collapse.

'The church tower?' he asked, wheezing only slightly, and more to Lucy and Col than the vicar.

'Sir Hezekiah Tower,' said the vicar. 'You've heard of him, of course?'

Col and Lucy turned to Stones. He shrugged. 'I'm not great with names.'

The vicar took a deep breath. 'Apart from Winston

Churchill and James Wolfe, of course, Sir Hezekiah Tower is one of the most celebrated former residents of Westerham.'

She paused here for Stones to chip in with more information. He did not.

'Alive in the late seventeenth, early eighteenth century, he made his fortune from lenses, perfecting a way to produce accurate but durable ones. His tomb is in the churchyard.'

She looked at the three blank faces. 'You're not from around here, I take it?' She walked across to a wooden table that was positioned next to the entrance. 'There are some leaflets. As I said, we're lacking wealthy parishioners, so if you were able to make a donation, we have one of those contactless machines. Is that what you call them? Machines? I don't know. Perhaps you have rich relatives? An inheritance?'

'You said Tower has a tomb outside?' asked Stones, doing a very bad job of disguising his excitement.

'Yes,' said the vicar, narrowing her eyes. 'You can't miss it. It's immediately opposite the front gate. It's the largest we've got. It even has a marble sword. These men and their weapons.' She paused. 'But it's all very fragile, so if you do want to have a look at it, please keep your distance. And remember . . . this is a consecrated site. Please respect the remains of our brethren, people. You know, we get *all* sorts in the graveyard. More often than not using it as a short cut. So don't *touch* the tomb.'

CHAPTER 37

Before touching the tomb, they waited on the path, showing mock respect as the vicar locked up the church and left. She was headed to The George and Dragon for a very late lunch ('Or is it early dinner?').

As soon as she'd stepped out of the front gate, Col was put 'on guard' as Lucy and Stones scrambled past gravestones to get to Sir Hezekiah Tower's massive and obvious tomb. It was the colour of ancient teeth and sat so distinct from the surrounding graves that it might have fallen from the sky.

Clouds had rolled across the earlier blue sky, casting grey shadows upon the graveyard.

'Dog walkers!' Stones shouted from the tomb. 'Keep

alert. Particularly for the older ones. Don't let them start chatting.'

Col didn't need to be told this. In fact, his stomach turned as he thought of Old Mrs Milton. It was a good job she walked her dog on the playing fields. If she caught them here, there'd be no chance of making the midnight deadline. Her chat would only be warming up by that point.

'And broadband engineers,' Lucy added in the tone of a primary-school teacher. 'Don't forget broadband engineers. Unless they're genuinely broadband engineers. And then they're fine. Fake broadband engineers. That's who you should watch out for. The pretend ones.'

Given how much he'd contributed to the day, it felt unfair to Col that he'd been allocated this role. Either of the others was capable of standing like a lonely gopher. I mean, they had eyes. In truth, his wasn't even a great lookout location. They were on the summit of the hill, fine, but the church blocked the view of the path they'd climbed earlier. To his right, the hill was so steep and the vegetation so verdant that you'd not be able to see walkers until they were pretty much in your face. And the church gate, off to the left, was heavy and more or less disguised people's entry until they'd creaked through.

He took a quick look over his shoulder towards the tomb. Stones's face was wet and red, and Lucy stared back at Col with an expression that he interpreted as 'help me'. The golf bag lay on the dandelion-covered grass.

'It's no good,' gasped Stones. 'It won't move.'

Like graverobbers, they'd been trying to push the lid off the tomb, a thick slab of marble that extended over the sides like a tabletop. Instinctively, Col knew this to be a mistake. Well, it was either instinct or gleaned from the few horror films he'd seen. The day had been difficult enough without releasing evil spirits.

'You can't be opening tombs!' he said, tiptoeing past graves to join them.

And, despite there being nobody around, Stones lifted a finger to his lips.

'He doesn't want the ghosts to hear,' said Lucy.

'You never know who's listening, Luce.'

'What does that mean?'

Stones thought for a moment. 'I don't know. But there are certain things you shouldn't be saying in a cemetery.'

He gripped the marble slab and tried shifting it again. The muscles in his neck looked like they'd pop before the stone moved. Which it didn't. Not even a millimetre.

'And there are things you shouldn't be *doing* in a cemetery,' whispered Col. 'Anyway, I thought the sword was meant to be, like, Dark Ages or something. Like *really* old.'

'It is,' said Stones.

'Didn't the vicar say this dude died in the eighteenth century?'

A shadow of sadness passed over Stones's face. It was, perhaps, the first time that Col wondered whether Dr Stones knew what he was doing, whether they'd actually ever manage to return the sword.

'*Dude?*' said Lucy.

Stones pointed at the inscription on the side of the tomb. The name Sir Hezekiah Tower was recognisable and after that lots of Latin. And then his dates: 1676–1745.

'A long life for back then.'

'So shouldn't we leave him be?' asked Col.

'There may be a clue in the tomb. Remember the windows, the letters? We're not disturbing his remains for the sake of it. It's what he would have wanted.'

'Don't forget the imminent end of the world,' said Lucy, somehow making it sound like an after-school club. 'Don't forget that.'

Underneath the dates was a marble sword. It wasn't a carving, but rather stood out from the flat surface of the marble. And, although it wasn't that similar to *the* sword, there was something . . . unusual about it.

'Look,' said Col.

'We've all seen the sword, eagle eyes.'

'No!'

Col sank to his knees. He traced a finger round the weapon. There was definitely something *different* about it, distinct from the surrounding stone. There! A crack ran between it and the side of the tomb. It hadn't been carved from the same marble block.

'Dog walker!' called Lucy. Too loudly. Loud enough for the dog walker to hear. For the dog walker to hold up a hand in greeting. And for Col to jump in surprise and topple forward and place both hands on the sword with all his weight to catch his balance.

And, would you believe it, but the sword moved. Initially Col thought he'd broken the thing, that somehow he'd snapped it off the tomb. But no. It slipped slowly down, keeping parallel to the tomb's straight lines because – get this! – the movement revealed it to be attached by metal rods in grooves.

'Wait! Don't move a muscle!' hissed Stones.

Col didn't entirely obey this instruction. He looked up at Lucy's dad, who leant on the tomb-top with one elbow. With his free hand, Stones waved at the passing dog walker.

'A long-lost relative!' he called, wearing the fakest smile ever.

As clear as day, the dog walker wasn't convinced. But he didn't stop, and he didn't ask questions. He just shook his head in that way dog walkers do and disappeared out of the gate and into the town.

Phew.

It's difficult to describe clearly what happened next. Col couldn't believe his eyes and wondered, again, whether all this might be a dream, and he was *actually* in bed recovering from banging his head after falling out of the window.

Let's take what happened next step by step.

First, Stones stopped waving. Then he pushed the brim of his hat back from his forehead in a gesture of exhaustion. Next he stopped leaning on the tomb and instead placed both palms on top of it. It was the kind of pose a general might adopt when looking at a table covered with maps. And slowly but clearly the tomb moved. To begin with, Col thought that the earlier fussing must have loosened the top. But then he saw that it wasn't only the top of the tomb that turned.

The whole structure split in two, a bit like a Lego model in the way it opened. The top end and the long side closest to Col stayed still as the other two sides gently moved away. There were hinges somewhere. It was designed to do this. They hadn't broken it. They'd found a hidden mechanism, a secret opening.

Despite the tomb splitting slowly, as if on gears, Stones was caught off balance and fell, his head missing a gravestone by mere centimetres. Lucy and Col skipped round to see what had been revealed.

Col took a deep breath, fearing the worst. He was too tired to cope with skeletons. But there were no bones. Instead there was a set of brick steps leading down into darkness.

Lucy looked at Col, and Col looked at Lucy. Before Stones had got up from the ground, Lucy was stepping into the gaping hole, with Col close behind.

CHAPTER
38

There were no skeletons. There were no zombies. There were no monsters of any kind, not even a broadband engineer or someone's uncle dressed in armour. There *was* a switch, which Lucy found at the bottom of the stairs, and, yes, she gasped when the strip lights flickered on, their stutter casting electric shadows like old-style photo negatives. It was a gasp of expectation, though, a gasp that seemed appropriate given the drama of the moment. Because they *had* found a secret passage accessible through a fake tomb. Surely this would lead to adventure or, at the very least, some eerie cobwebs, etc?

The lights caught, revealing the room's contents. Two stacks of plastic moulded chairs that were orange and a *bit* dusty. Some cardboard boxes too, full of books not bones, blue and probably containing hymns. There was a thin table that didn't look very safe, with foldable legs, the sort you might paste wallpaper on. A broom leant sadly against it. This underground chamber, the day's second, was the size of a classroom and about as exciting too (i.e. not very; keep up at the back). The walls were brick, and in the corner of the room there was a wooden door. It felt very much like a storeroom.

'Wait for me, kids!' called Stones. 'Who knows what danger . . .'

He bundled into them at the bottom of the stairs. There was no point in finishing his sentence.

'It doesn't look much like an ancient burial ground, Dad,' said Lucy. 'Unless the warrior wanted to spend eternity with plastic chairs and cardboard boxes.'

Stones wasn't able to tell his daughter off for her unceasing saltiness because there came a sound of grinding stone and squeaking metal. All three realised immediately what this was: Tower's tomb was closing. Col darted up the steps, but arrived only to see the white sliver of light disappear as the mechanism completed its turns, the stones coming together with a thud of finality. Lucy joined him and, soon after, her dad did too, slightly out of breath.

The light from downstairs struggled to reach up here. They ran their blind hands over the brickwork, desperate for a release lever, a knob of hope.

'There must be one!' said Stones. 'How else will we get out?'

All they found was brick. And a worm. Which made Col scream. Because he accidentally squashed it, and his hands got covered in worm juice, and I don't need to tell you how unpleasant that was.

'Isn't there another door downstairs?' said Lucy.

Moving as one again, they half tumbled, half flew down the steps and across the room. And, yes, there *was* a handle that belonged to a door and, yes, Lucy pulled it and pulled it and pulled it some more . . . but the door wouldn't budge.

'Maybe it's a push,' suggested Col, wiping his wormy hands down his tracksuit bottoms.

'Thanks, genius,' said Lucy and put her shoulder to the door, but this did nothing either.

'Stand aside, children,' said Stones.

He spent a good few minutes trying to open it. But it was obviously locked. Short of finding a key to fit the hole beneath the handle, there wasn't really very much they could do.

Stones lifted three chairs from a stack. He sat down in one, dejected. Even the brim of his hat seemed floppier than before. Lucy joined him. Col continued standing, worried that taking a seat indicated an acceptance of defeat.

'I guess that's that, then,' said Lucy, looking at her father for words of reassurance, a sign that all was not lost.

Col tried the handle again, pulling with all his might. Doors had been forced in the past. Anyone who's ever watched movies knows that the police are *always* doing it. They use those thick cylinders of metal. He looked around the room. What if there were a fire extinguisher? That'd be perfect. A swing and a smash. Job done.

His eyes darted from table to chairs to boxes, from corner to corner. But there were no fire extinguishers. There was nothing even vaguely like a fire extinguisher. The broom maybe. Was that like a fire extinguisher? No. Of course not. What was he thinking?

Sometimes, if the police didn't have the smashy cylindrical things, they used their feet. Again Col knew this to be true because he'd seen it on TV. They kicked doors down. Just like that. Bang. Sometimes they weren't even wearing big boots.

And so Col stepped back from the door. He sized it up. The lock was at a kickable height. He'd not be smashing it like a football, but using his heel as in karate. It wasn't about strength but precision. He thought back to his attack on Ross's privates. This was a new skill unlocked today. He could kick well. He was a kicker.

He took three steps back. He wiped his forehead. He attacked the door.

He *was* successful in striking the exact part he'd been aiming for. He did so with some force too. You'd have been impressed if you'd been watching. And the door shook, as if scared, and a shotgun sound of impact tremored across the room.

Col, new at this kicking-down-doors business, slipped and fell backwards, his head striking the unforgiving floor with an unpleasant crack. He was okay, though. At least he didn't want to show Lucy that it hurt. He scrambled to his feet and was presented with a door that looked pretty much exactly how it had done a minute earlier, albeit with a black scuff mark below the lock.

He was growing to dislike this door.

Lucy and Stones had turned their heads on hearing the kick noise. This, however, was as far as their interest went. Lucy didn't even bother with any snark. They sympathised with Col. After all, they wanted to escape too.

'This,' said Lucy, shrugging at the room. 'Is this it?'

'Many famous thinkers have asked the same question,' said Stones sadly. On seeing Lucy's frowning reaction, however, he added, 'I'm sorry. Not the time.'

Col, rubbing his head, but in a way that didn't suggest extreme pain, returned to the steps. Here Stones had rested the golf bag in his first moments of disappointment. Col whipped off the protective sock. He pulled out the sword. It wasn't the magical moment when a hero reveals an awesome weapon from their scabbard because its handle got caught against the bag's straps, but it was still pretty cool. There was something about the strip lighting down here that really showed off the elegant turns of the runic script that danced along the silver blade.

Col hadn't removed the sword to admire it, though. Brandishing it as if to chop off the head of some ridiculously mean dragon, he marched back to the locked door, aka his sworn enemy.

'Col,' sighed Stones. 'Whatever you're thinking of doing, don't.'

Col didn't listen, though. If he'd learnt anything in the last few days, it was to trust his instincts and to ignore adults. First off, he thrust the sword in a stabbing motion at the door. Jab. And if the door had been alive it would definitely be hurting.

It wasn't, though. And, in all fairness, he probably hadn't given this enough thought. Even if the blade *had* passed through the wood, which it very much did not, it wouldn't have made the door any more open. As it was, the tip left a tiny indentation, the kind of dent that a careless football boot might inflict upon a skirting board.

Lucy let out a little shriek. But she wasn't scared. She was laughing. That was something, thought Col. At least he was keeping spirits up.

He cleared his throat. He wasn't done yet. 'You just wait,' he said.

Next he raised the sword over his right shoulder to ready himself for a downward slicing motion. The stabbing attempt had been a mistake. The situation called for ULTRAVIOLENCE.

'It's a priceless artefact,' said Stones. 'You'll damage the thing!'

But Col paid no heed. The way he saw it, the sword was a weapon designed for destruction, not admiration. Hadn't its owner been a warrior? Warriors famously hate doors.

Readying himself, Col visualised a door-free future. Col visualised himself. Col: Destroyer of Doors.

And down he chopped. A little. Because the door stopped much of the planned chopping. The blade scored a faint line where it had touched the wood. And nothing much else happened. And it was only a scratch.

Reader, the chopping had failed.

CHAPTER 39

Col was a kid. He was weak. An adult, a strong(ish) adult, could do better surely? Why hadn't Stones tried shouldering the door? People shouldered doors all the time. This was the problem with being a Doctor of Literature: no practical skills; a lack of shoulder use.

'Come and sit down,' said Stones. 'You'll tire yourself out.'

Lucy smiled, and the chair looked so inviting that, yes, Col thought he *would* give himself a quick break. But that didn't mean that he'd given up with the smashing-through-the-door-with-a-sword plan. I mean, thinking back to the video games he played, his characters were *always* smashing through doors with swords. If only it were as easy as a couple of taps of the controller. He'd tried stabbing and chopping. What other motions were there? Could he use the sword like a crowbar? Would that work?

Col sat with the sword across his thighs. It felt strangely heavier in that position, not the lightweight sweeping steel when he brandished it more traditionally. He'd have to be careful not to stand up too quickly for fear of doing himself an injury.

'You know,' said Stones, 'I was convinced that we'd solved the mystery. The sword in the church window, the letters, the anagram, the tower. And –' he gestured towards the brick steps – 'a secret passage accessible through a tomb. It's all so perfect. I didn't think for a minute that we'd end up locked in a storeroom.' He looked at Lucy. 'Didn't you say the sword was meant to bring luck?'

She stretched over to pat her father on the leg. Col offered a muted smile. He dropped his eyes to the sword and once more admired its craftsmanship. You'd not think it possible that something so delicately made but robust – it was weighty like it meant business, but curved with the subtlety of a raindrop – could have been forged so many hundreds of years ago. He could understand why people paid big money for beautiful things. He could understand why museums wanted to display beautiful things. They stood out, did beautiful things, from the grey of the everyday.

'Maybe,' said Col, continuing to look at the sword, 'it didn't mean Tower the man. Maybe it meant another tower?'

'The church tower, you mean? Built on the site of the ancient burial. Yes, I thought that too.'

Such was the excitement in Stones's voice that Col looked over at him. It was amazing how little it had taken to reignite the fire in his eyes. The man was either mad or genuinely believed the fate of the world rested on returning the sword in time.

Lucy's head was bowed as she picked at her fingers.

'The thing about the apocalypse,' she said, 'is that it's happening now. Climate change, people. So, you know, if we *don't* manage to return the sword in time, it's no biggie . . . I'm trying to cheer us up!'

The thought came to Col as if communicated to him through his fingertips. That's what he'd tell you if you asked him about it. It was as if the sword *whispered* through him. It sounds strange. But that's because it *was* strange.

(And, remember this: he'd been through a lot that day. A tired mind can't be trusted.)

'Or the tower in the woods?' he suggested.

'What tower?' said Stones and Lucy at exactly the same time.

'The tower in Tower Wood. That's why it's called Tower Wood?' The two stared at him in disbelief. 'Because there's a tower there . . .'

It wasn't the name that shocked them. It was more that Col hadn't thought to mention this earlier. Stones asked him exactly this question.

'Well . . . it all happened so quickly. The vicar and the tomb and, like you say, the whole moving sword and secret passage. I didn't really have time to think.'

Tower Wood was a spread of pine trees on the edge of town. At their very centre was a ruined tower – set back, away from any path, meaning you had to know where you were going to spot its blurred angles through the trees. And you'd better wear trousers because there were thorns and stinging nettles everywhere.

'And the weird thing,' said Col, exactly as he always told anyone who didn't know about the tower, 'is that it looks like a skull.'

Okay, so, yes, it does look a bit like a skull. But in the same way that cloud formations *sometimes* resemble dinosaurs or puppies or alien spaceships. It requires some suspension of disbelief and a lot of squinting to see how the broken entrance might be a mouth. The circular windows towards the top were, perhaps, eye-like. But the building was shaped like a tower, not a head. And it was ruined too – the seizing ivy, which covered most of the ancient brick, having pulled down one side and the roof. Beams that separated the space into two floors were long gone too. In conclusion, it looked a *little* like a skull, but far more like a ruined tower.

Nobody knows why it was there. Nobody knows why it was allowed to crumble. Was it a hunting lodge? A lookout? Was it built to appear like a ruin, something that the local landowner could use to make his lands feel all the more mysterious? Who knows? But it was there now. And it was definitely a tower.

(Col explained all this, but made more of its resemblance to a skull.)

'*And* it's on this little mound too.'

'A mound?' said Stones. 'Like a *burial* mound?'

'I guess,' said Col, although in truth it was difficult to say because it was hard to judge how mound-y the mound was, seeing as it was covered in stinging nettles and blackberry bushes and the rest. And also Col wasn't entirely sure what a burial mound was.

'Right!' Stones stood up. 'We'd better get going! Stand back, children!'

He eyed the door as if it had said something nasty about his mother. Col felt a wave of fuzzy affection, almost like Stones was going to sort out some big kid who'd been a bully.

The Doctor of Literature showed his shoulder to the door. And took four bounding steps towards it.

Finally, thought Col.

But his shoulder had about the same impact as a toddler attempting to push a juggernaut: absolutely none.

Stones stood back and rubbed his arm, slight confusion clouding his features.

'It's definitely locked,' he said.

'You don't say,' said Lucy.

Stones turned to her, his heels squeaking against the floor. His eyebrows were low in irritation. Already he'd forgotten his sore shoulder.

'Well, what do you suggest?' he said. 'It's all very well carping from the sidelines.'

'How about we scream?' she said. 'Who knows? Maybe the vicar's back from dinner? Maybe a dog walker will hear us? Maybe there's someone on the other side?'

One eyebrow drifted upwards. 'I hadn't considered

that,' he said and gestured to his daughter with a calming palm. 'But pause on the screaming for a sec.'

He approached the door once more. He cleared his throat. He raised a fist. He knocked three times, and they waited. There was no instant reaction.

(This wasn't massively surprising, to be honest.)

'How about we scream now?'

Stones raised a finger and cocked his head. He'd heard something.

'Listen!' he hissed.

And, yes, there was a noise. Definitely the sound of something. But not from the door. It was getting steadily crunchier and steadily louder, and it was soon obvious what was happening.

The tomb was opening!

'Someone's coming down!' whispered Lucy, grabbing her father's arm in fear.

Col didn't know whether to rush up the stairs or hide. He ended up doing neither, paralysed next to the boxes of blue hymnbooks. *It'll be fine*, he told himself. *It'll be the vicar. Or, at worst, a dog walker.* And he was about to say this to the others when he saw first the legs, then the waist, then the chest, then the hair, then the everything of the visitor.

This was not the vicar. This was not the dog walker. This was Dr Draco.

'We *must* stop meeting like this,' she purred.

CHAPTER
40

Col must have somehow given away what he was considering. The tomb, for whatever reason, hadn't closed behind Draco. You could see the glow of the afternoon's dying sunlight against the staircase wall. Already it had been a day *full* of running. His parents would be proud. All he needed to do was continue this by sprinting past Draco, and up and out, and bingo. He'd decide the next step of the plan when he was safely outside. It wasn't good to plot *too* far ahead.

But: 'Don't get any funny ideas about escaping, boy,' said Draco. 'I wouldn't want anyone to get hurt.' She stopped to consider what she'd said. 'Wow. I really do sound like a villain, don't I? I'd never really thought of myself like that before.'

'How did you know to come here?' asked Stones.

'There are a great many admirable things about you, *amore mio*. Or at least there were twenty years ago. But, and please don't take offence, you are one of the most singularly predictable people I've ever met. As soon as these children stole the sword—'

'*We* didn't steal the sword. *You* stole the sword,' said Lucy, arms tightly crossed.

Col felt like he should add something, so he did. In a mumble. 'Yeah, from my back garden.'

'Has your father not taught you that it's rude to interrupt when an adult's speaking?' Draco asked, a single eyebrow raised. 'As I was saying, as soon as these children stole the sword, I suspected you had a hand in it. And when one of my people reported seeing a man in a Panama hat running across the castle fields I knew I was right. You're not the only one to have read Amis's diaries. And what with your obsession with apocalyptic curses and –' she did air quotes – '*doing the right thing*, you'd want to be returning the sword. It's tedious, really.'

'I'm trying to save the world, Diana. You make it sound like I'm a trainspotter.'

Draco addressed the children. 'You don't believe any of this, do you? Ancient curses and magical weapons.

It's all so clichéd.' She dropped her voice and narrowed her eyes. 'That said, you've not suddenly become especially lucky, have you?'

They were saved from having to answer by Draco pulling a gun from her handbag, like it was nothing, like she'd drawn it a thousand times already. And, who knows, maybe she had? She let the red leather bag fall to the floor. Its bright colour stood out from the storeroom's monochrome.

'No matter. All it took was a quick chat with a dog walker to lead me to the tomb. If you three had a brain between you, you might be dangerous.'

The gun was an ornate thing, probably stolen from a museum, with a pearl handle and an octagonal barrel. It was more the kind of weapon that you might duel with. If, umm, you were ever called upon to duel. But it was still very much a gun, and the sight of it froze Col's lungs. In fact, it took a great deal of effort to continue breathing.

'Place the sword on the floor!' Draco shouted suddenly, her voice bouncing against the brick, her temper momentarily lost. 'The time for polite conversation is over!' Her voice returned to its usual calm control. 'You can tell because I'm pointing a gun at you.'

Col looked at Stones and Lucy. They both nodded

urgently. And so, despite feeling that he was making a huge mistake, Col bent down to lay the sword on the floor. Draco moved not a foot forward, her leg muscles, or internal clockwork, frozen. She gestured with her gun at the chairs.

'And sit down. All three of you.'

'Diana,' said Stones. 'Why are you doing this?'

Despite being in a room with someone holding a gun and despite the world quite possibly coming to an end pretty soon, Col thought of James Bond, Alex Rider, Minions; stories where the villain's only too happy to reveal their conspiracy, to unmask their motivation.

'Why does anyone do anything, Henry?' she said.

It took a while before Col realised that this was Stones's first name. It was strange he'd not heard it before.

'Money. It sounds a vulgar justification, but do you know how much it costs to run a historical re-enactment society? You'd not believe me if I told you. Cost-of-living crisis. The energy crisis. The crises mount up. Even when someone lets you use their castle for free. We can't be dreamers forever. At some point, we must realise the obvious: things cost money. And nice things cost even more. Academics aren't paid very much. Writers even less.'

'Why the ritual, then?'

She shrugged. 'Why not? I've always been a romantic.'

'You're no longer the person I knew,' said Stones, sitting down alongside Lucy and Col. 'Anything that might give you an advantage, you manipulate and exploit. What happened?'

'I matured,' she replied. 'You ought to give it a try.'

She kept the gun trained on them as she slid down to grab the sword. As ever, she moved in a sweeping motion, half machine, half dancer. Still, you could see the effort required to lift the weapon. It was strange that its weight appeared to depend on who held it.

'The police are after you, lady,' said Lucy as Draco straightened her back, gun in one hand, sword in the other, a maxed-out RPG character.

Draco's smiling response was forced and unconvincing, as if she'd tasted something foul at the exact time she was pretending to find a joke funny.

'You think a pair of idiot officers in an unmarked transit van are going to stop me? I'll be miles away by the time you three escape here. I'll find more children, Karen's two nieces, and by the end of the week a new ritual will be complete, the sword will be sold and I'll be free to start again, lucky or not. I'm thinking America. They love their history over there. Or should I say *our* history? Don't worry. I'll call someone to rescue you in the morning. I'm not a complete monster, regardless of what Henry tells you.'

'I never speak about you,' said Stones. 'Well, hardly ever.'

'Of course, my love,' said Draco. 'Of course.'

And, in another reality, all that Draco described *actually* happened. In this alternate universe, Rose the vicar didn't decide against another glass of wine with her late lunch/ early dinner. In this reality, she didn't remember that she'd forgotten to check on the spare hymnbooks that might be needed for Monday's massive funeral. She didn't return to the church. She didn't approach the 'Sir Hezekiah Tower storeroom' via the more traditional entrance. And she didn't put her key in the lock at the exact moment Draco took her first step back into the stairwell, about to make her escape.

But ours isn't a different reality. Ours is real life. Ours is what's happening in this story. And for Lucy, Stones and Col – well, they were all extremely *lucky*. But, then again, doesn't every happy present rely on a fortunate past?

'What's that? Who's that?' said Draco, frozen, her attention turned to the door.

The handle turned. The door opened into the room, disguising the visitor until the very last moment.

(So it *wasn't* a push, thought Col.)

And in stepped the vicar. She obviously hadn't heard Draco, and she didn't instantly see that the storeroom was occupied. Her head was down, and she was holding a phone. TikTok. Amusing dogs. And it was Col scraping a foot that caught her attention. And she jumped, almost dropping the phone, and put a hand to her chest.

'Goodness me,' she said. 'You gave me such a fright.' She looked at Lucy and Stones. 'I'm assuming you found our secret entrance. I should put a panic button in this room, I really should, the amount of people who end up trapped in here. If I've told Terry once, I've told him a thousand times to block the mechanism, to shut up the hole. But he's a quirky fellow and thinks it's useful in case we ever forget the church keys. Which is nonsense, of course, because you need a key to get through *this* door.' And, as her gaze fell on Draco and in particular the gun, she continued speaking in the exact same tone, offering no surprise or fear. 'And I see you're pointing a gun at me. I'm sorry, I don't think we've met.'

Draco smiled. Once more, it looked like an expression designed by algorithm.

'I'm afraid you've walked into someone else's nightmare, Your Holiness,' said Draco. 'What I suggest you do is return from whence you came and say nothing about what you've seen. Amen.'

'Oh,' said Rosie, not moving. 'Well, I hope there won't be any unpleasantness here. It's holy ground, you see. Or holy underground.'

Draco nodded. 'If all parties play along –' she turned to look pointedly at Stones – 'I promise there will be no *unpleasantness*. And, you never know, a few days from now, the church might receive a donation, a thank-you gift, if you understand what I'm saying, which I very much hope that you do. I just *love* the colour of your cardigan, by the way.'

Rosie looked from Lucy to Stones to Col. She said nothing, but returned her phone to a pocket. Slowly and silently, she turned and headed back towards the door.

'Please!' said Lucy.

But Rosie passed through the door and it closed behind her, and they heard the tick-tock of the lock and that was that, it seemed.

'Now,' said Draco. 'Where were we?'

But before anyone could answer a voice sounded. And the voice belonged to the vicar.

'Don't worry, everyone!' she said, calling through the door. 'I'm ringing the police as we speak! Pointing a gun at a woman of the cloth! The very cheek of it.'

At this, Col became a standing stone in a stream of action.

As Draco stepped towards the door, face creased in frustration, Lucy sprang from her chair. She didn't dive for the doctor, but instead headed for the table and, in particular, its broom.

Draco turned at this sudden movement and, in doing so, fired the gun. But, as she'd earlier asserted, she *wasn't* a monster. She'd shot in panic: she hadn't *meant* to pull the trigger. The explosion filled the room, its blast ringing in everyone's ears. Stones and Col instinctively covered theirs. But not Lucy.

She'd grabbed the broomstick and, holding it as near as possible to how she'd been taught in fencing class, she thrust the end at Draco. And in particular Draco's hand. And in particular the gun, smoke rising from its barrel like a tiny ghost.

Smack! She knocked it from the woman's grip. It bounced against the floor and presumably – but Col couldn't be sure because his hearing was only just returning – made a metallic crack as it did so.

Draco, shocked into action, grabbed at Lucy's broom, swinging it sideways. Grunting like wrestlers, the two faced each other with the wooden stick between their chests, pushing and pulling to gain advantage. And, yes, Draco was older and possessed a wiry strength, but Lucy was determined. Lucy was angry. Just look at her face, tight with willpower, teeth clamped in fortitude. Col shook to help her, but by the time he'd persuaded his legs to move it was all over.

And here's the thing: Lucy might possibly have won . . . if not for her dad and his groaning.

She turned her head to see him holding his calf tightly. And she saw the blood soaking a crimson circle through his trousers, just above the ankle. Lucy gasped, and as she did so Draco pushed violently against the broom, forcing Lucy to lose her grip, knocking the girl to the floor.

She fell with a bang – a noise Col realised he could actually hear, which was something, at least.

'See what you've done?' called Draco, hair alive with anger. 'See where your meddling's left you? Vicar! Can you hear me? The gun's gone off! Someone's been hit!'

'It's nothing,' said Stones. 'I've had worse.'

He was grimacing horribly, though, like a model for

a test that determined whether you could judge if someone was in immense pain.

Draco's anger vanished. 'Oh, Henry!' she said, adopting a more sympathetic tone, perhaps provoked by the disturbing white of Stones's face.

And there, at Col's feet, just begging to be lifted, was the sword.

CHAPTER
41

'Look!' said Lucy, pointing to the floor.

Col lifted his eyes from the sword and followed Lucy's finger. But already Draco was bending down to retrieve the bullet. It looked like a large ball bearing and was grey and nothing like Col had imagined it would be.

'Did it pass through you?' Draco asked Stones, again seemingly concerned.

He frowned, colour returning to his face. He pulled up his trouser leg. There was a mark, sure enough, and it *was* bleeding. But it looked more a scratch than a shooting injury. Col had suffered worse in Year Five when his parents had forced him to attend the after-school soccer skills academy for a term. Stones winced as he unrolled his bloody trouser leg.

'I said it wasn't a big deal. It's just a nick.'

'You were lucky, Dad,' said Lucy, looking relieved.

'Idiots,' muttered Draco. 'Everywhere I go: idiots. I thought I'd *shot* you, Henry.'

Then she turned, and it was obvious what was in her mind. The police were coming, if the vicar were to be believed. She should grab the sword and flee. I mean, that's what *you'd* do, right?

Col saw that he could stop her by simply taking the sword. The gun was no longer a threat. It was off in the corner and, by the look of it, so old that it fired only a single shot before needing to be reloaded.

Bravery, that's what was required. Or stupidity. One or the other. Col wasn't entirely sure how they were different.

There was a split second when Col and Draco stood poised on either side of the fallen sword, almost as if they were waiting for an umpire to fire a starting pistol.

It was Lucy who broke their trance. '*Get it, Col!*'

And Col dived, and maybe it was his recent experience of falling that saw him get his fingertips to the sword first but, whatever the reason, he did, and he also performed a sick sideways roll that took him away from Draco's own desperate grasp. In truth, he scraped his knees a little, and if you'd been studying his face extremely closely you'd have seen him wince. But the momentum enabled him (more by luck than judgement) to sweep up on to his feet and so come to a stop with his back to the exit stairs and the sword held out as if he really knew what he was doing, like an Absolute Lad.

A quick glance at Lucy and, yes, she was impressed enough to clap her hands in joy, which was completely un-Lucy-like, but his balloon of self-satisfaction was burst by Draco laughing, actually laughing, which was a snide and hurtful thing to do. She picked up the broomstick. She took a threatening step forward.

'What's going on in there? You're awfully quiet. The police will arrive soon,' squeaked Rosie from behind the door. 'Is someone *still* shot?'

The police were bad news for Draco, but they weren't much better for the continued existence of the world either. Even if Stones managed to explain the whole situation, even if Col chipped in with the revelation that the sword had been dug up from *his* garden, the police would be unlikely to let them take it away for reburial. Especially not by midnight.

'Give it to me,' said Draco, jabbing the stick at Col's face with each word. Every time, he dodged it, but only just. 'I don't want to hurt anyone else. I don't *enjoy* hurting people. Ask Henry.'

'You broke my heart!' murmured Stones.

'Not now, Dad,' said Lucy with a sigh like a deflating bouncy castle.

Despite Draco's claim, a wide grin spread across her face. She raised the stick high, looking for all the world not only as if she were about to hit Col, but also like she was totally into it.

Col did what any of us would do in the same situation, especially if we were holding a sword. He lifted the weapon to protect himself.

'Oh!' said Draco, pausing her attack. 'You want to fight, do you? I fenced for my university, I'll have you know. My lunge was the talk of the campus.'

And, although it sounded like she was boasting about garden improvement, Col couldn't help but gulp. Sure, if you find a sword that bad guys are after, you're probably going to end up taking part in a sword fight at some point – he understood this – but he'd rather hoped that Dr Stones might have been the one shouting, '*En garde!*', or whatever you're meant to say.

(But maybe, in life as much as in sword-fighting, it's more important to *look* like you know what you're doing.)

Despite what Draco had learnt at university, however, she obviously enjoyed playing dirty. She didn't step back. She didn't offer Col a pause to compose his trembling thoughts and shaking muscles. No. She simply continued with her downward thrust.

He lifted the sword to parry the attack. It struck the broomstick's halfway point. And, as easy as a spoon through jelly, it broke the stick. Draco now held two bits of wood, both with ends that were dramatically more jagged and threatening than the original.

She brushed bright hair from her eyes with the crook of her arm. She stood ready for further combat. Col licked his lips and tried to look mean but failed. His knees were still sore from the earlier scraping, and he suddenly needed the toilet, which was probably nerves. The air in the room was light and hot, and that didn't help either, to be honest.

Col tried focusing his thoughts. Here was a moment for a joke, a dope witticism. But what could he say? He'd been thrust into this role without preparation or permission. What he really needed was a scriptwriter.

And as he was about to say, 'Nobody messes with Col Coleridge!', which, in hindsight, would have been pretty much the lamest thing in history, his opponent,

Dr Draco, was suddenly bundled to the floor by a leaping combination of father and daughter.

The three bodies rolled around, almost like puppies play-fighting, but with Draco's flashing hair making it look like they were on fire.

If Col's mum had been present, she'd have definitely warned them about the danger of the pointy sticks and how they'd have someone's eye out. But she wasn't, so Col stepped forward, wondering if he should try to slap Draco with the flat side of the sword if he got the chance. Her dark dress rolled past in fabric bursts against Stones's white linen shirt and Lucy's more conventional activewear.

The sticks clattered away, lost in Draco's attempt to free herself from her attackers. Stones's head emerged from under an armpit. He spat out his words.

'Run, Col! Close the tomb behind you! Save the world!'

And I'd be lying if I said Col left instantly. He hesitated. It took a glare from Lucy, whose hair was being pulled in a most unsporting way, and the words, 'What are you waiting for?' to get him moving, clutching the sword and racing up the clattering stone steps.

CHAPTER 42

Broadband engineers everywhere. Roaming in pairs like neon swans. Which either meant that Westerham was finally going to get decent broadband, or that Draco, before descending into the storeroom, had ordered them out on patrol.

After leaving the tomb, Col had kicked away the rock used by Draco to jam the mechanism. Her call of, '*Nooooo!*' had leaked from the stairs until silenced by the stone edges of the tomb coming together, the passage closing with a soft thud. With the sword merrily glittering, Col checked for nearby vicars or nosy dog walkers (there were none) and stepped away, heading for the churchyard gate and the next stage of his journey.

He didn't enjoy a *completely* smooth escape from the

graves. One: he knocked a knee against a listing tombstone, and the pain reminded him that his legs still hurt from the earlier grazing. (At least his ankle was feeling better.) His cheek, as if jealous of the attention given to his knees, also throbbed in pain. And two: a pair of yellow-jacketed broadband engineers emerged from round the side of the church.

Col hid behind a useful nearby tree, positioning, with extra caution, the sword behind him. He could well have stood in the centre of the path, though, for the amount of attention the two paid to their surroundings. Both had their heads down, and both were studying their phones. Either the devices contained information pertinent to their search, or the engineers were mad for social media. Col watched them leave the graveyard and, after checking left and right for dog walkers, he followed.

He paused, only a few steps from the church gate, waiting for another couple of yellow jackets to pass the bus stop down on the main road.

A glance over his shoulder revealed that the road-walking engineers were far enough away. Go! He quick-stepped across the grass, doing his best to keep the sword subtle, which is easier said than done, wishing that he'd brought Stones's golf bag.

Not for the first time that afternoon, Col was lucky. There was no traffic on the main road, and he crossed without breaking stride. On the other side were steps leading to a shadowy path between two houses. He'd been down here more times than he could remember: it was the trail to Tower Wood, the route his parents liked to take when they'd decided, as they did every so often, that a family walk was a good idea. Disappearing into the shade, he allowed himself another look back. The angle wasn't particularly revealing, but it did show that he wasn't being chased by any engineers. Well, there weren't any *immediately* behind him.

'Lovely sword,' said an elderly man with large glasses, surprising Col with his sudden appearance, a fluffy white dog panting at his knees.

'Thanks,' said Col automatically.

The man didn't stop, thank goodness, and Col continued too, in the opposite direction, forcing quicker steps. In time, the houses' walls gave way to fences and the overhanging branches of garden trees. He wondered whether he should hide the sword in his tracksuit bottoms. It was only a *bit* longer than his legs, and if he stuck it down one, the hilt resting on his waistband, he *might* be able to disguise it. Obviously he'd have to walk without bending his knee. Also, he'd need to ensure the sharp point didn't cut his foot off or – worse because of his parents' reaction – damage a trainer.

Col decided to save this option for later. If he bumped into any more dog walkers, he *might* try hiding it. He'd grown to learn how dangerous dog walkers were. They were like a network of secret agents.

He thought of Lucy. He thought of leaving her behind. Was that . . . bad? She'd be fine, wouldn't she? Yes. She didn't need his help, didn't need the help of a magical sword. She was Lucy. She was strong. She was . . . a friend. He sucked at his bottom lip. She'd be fine. She'd be fine. As long as he saved the world.

The path ended at a kissing gate, surrounded on each side by huge tangles of brambles. Col passed through and out into a steep meadow of rough grass. This was where he'd bring a sledge when it snowed. Little did he know, in winters past, that one day he'd be returning to save the world . . . or whatever it was that he was now doing.

He rested the sword on his shoulder and headed for the pine forest that lay over the hill's crest. He tried thinking of other things. He tried thinking of nothing. It would soon be school, meaning that if he failed to prevent the apocalypse at least he'd miss the start of the new academic year, which wouldn't be the end of the world, so to speak.

He remembered the relay race. If he hadn't frozen, if he'd won the thing for his family, would he be here now? Had his parents been right all along about the importance of athletics?

He checked his watch. It was past six, later than he'd thought. How long to reach the tower? Ten minutes? Fifteen? It was a good job he'd escaped the storeroom when he had. They might have been trapped in there all night. Or even a police cell. Imagine that. What would his parents say? He hoped Lucy and her dad were okay.

And as he walked, careful not to trip over a sudden thistle for fear of chopping off his head, he turned to worrying about the practicalities of what faced him. Stones suspected the tower was built on a burial mound, which meant that Col had to *bury* the sword there. Fine. But how would he know *exactly* where? Would there be a sign? What if he dug in the wrong place? And also would he have to deal with skeletons? Or worms? And anyway, before any of this, he wasn't even sure *how* he was meant to dig. He had the vague idea of using the sword to cut into the ground somehow but, thinking back to summers on the beach and the hours it took to excavate a few buckets' worth of sand, he wasn't entirely sure that would work.

The incline of the meadow, now more a hill than a field, began to get to his legs. His face too, keen not to be forgotten, began to sweat something silly, which in no way helped with the wound situation. If Col had had his phone, he'd have been able to Google. Google what exactly, he wasn't sure, but there was bound to be *some* useful information out there.

Still, even though he wasn't convinced about the whole end-of-the-world thing, his luck *had* improved since his face had been scratched by the sword. And so he continued walking, hopeful, in a desperate kind of way, that something, anything, would reveal itself once he arrived at the tower.

(And *not* a broadband engineer or a Dr Draco.)

CHAPTER 43

Okay, so Col got lost, and if it were him telling you this story, and not me, he'd leave that detail out. But, in his defence, the thing about pine forests is that you can be walking between the light brown trunks, over the crunching needles, kicking pinecones away, and it *feels* like you're making progress, but on every side are the selfsame trees, and you may well have been running on the spot for all the difference your movement's made to your surroundings. What I'm trying to say is that it's easy to lose your bearings here.

Col's mistake, and he'd admit it himself, was leaving the path. (Never leave the path.) Admittedly, it was a short cut, but only if he'd definitely known where he should have been heading, which he didn't. And, as the pine trees led to further pine trees, and through the pine trees he could only see more pine trees, he wondered what had happened to all that good luck.

He yawned. A miserable sound. It'd been a long day.

Up ahead was a fallen tree. Col welcomed this because a) he didn't think he'd passed it already and b) it was nice to see a little variation. He wandered over and sat down, his knees aching only slightly, and placed the tip of the sword in the ground and rested his hands on the hilt. On top of his hands he laid his chin. He noticed how the sword sank a little. Did this mean the ground was soft? If he ever reached the tower, that was good news. It was a *positive*.

Even with the end of the world, though, he didn't fancy digging. It was challenging work. There was a reason why all the broadband engineers looked so big. They needed muscles for their spadework. If it hadn't been the world he needed to save, if he was doing it to spare Tunbridge Wells, say, Col would have serious doubts about going through with it. As long as everyone in Tunbridge Wells was saved. He wasn't a monster. Not like Dr Draco.

He lightly touched the cut on his cheek. It had scabbed over and was less sore. He half wished it would leave a scar. Lucy said he'd look badass. Like a pirate. A proper badass pirate.

Right. Let's think options. The obvious one was to turn round and retrace his steps to the path. The only problem with this, though, was that Col didn't know which way he'd come, what with all the trees, and therefore what 'turning round' might actually entail. (Also, he'd never been good with angles.)

A sudden noise – it was hard to judge where from, but it was a pigeon flapping its wings in panic, rising from the wood – disturbed the silence. If Col could fly, that would make things easier.

That he didn't have his phone wasn't a huge problem, not for now anyway. Part of the reason he hated walks in Tower Wood was that the reception was so bad. Google Maps would be useless. Still, he could have taken some sick selfies with him and the sword, etc.

Another option: he could continue walking. Either he'd reach the tower, or the wood would end. Because it wasn't an infinite wood. He'd have definitely heard about it if that were the case. Yes, carrying on walking was a decent choice. It was just a shame, and his chest tightened when he considered this, that the deadline was creeping closer and closer and he'd still not buried the sword.

He looked up and tried to identify where the sun was shining from. This was difficult. Not least because the earlier clouds still remained *and* he was having to peer through the high branches. It seemed a bit brighter in one direction, above the stick that looked like a gun. The tower was north from the town. If he could only remember whether the sun set in the east or the west, he might be able to decide which was the best direction to take.

Bums.

Col stood up, pushing the sword further into the ground. He pulled it out easily enough, though, and it looked like he'd managed to kill *another* worm (they certainly weren't having great luck today). A long sigh. After everything he'd gone through . . . to find himself lost in the woods.

He was an idiot – that's the thing. Lucy and her dad hadn't known him long enough to realise. He was someone who froze during relay races, who fell out of windows. A massive idiot. Letting everyone down again. And, by *everyone*, he really did mean *everyone*. (His eyes softened with tears.)

What was he thinking? He should lie down and forget about it all and wait for a dog walker or the police or whatever because it wasn't like *he* was going to save anything or anyone. A hero? Ha! A *zero* more like.

There came another sound. Another bird. Col wiped his forearm across his nose. But it *wasn't* a bird because he could see someone moving through the trees, a dark figure, distant but getting closer, disappearing behind a trunk before reappearing at a closer one.

He'd stop feeling sorry for himself. For now. His heart hadn't really been in it anyway.

Was it Draco? No. You'd notice her hair from a mile off. He could see who it was. The round-shouldered walk, moving almost . . . sarcastically.

OMG.

'Lucy!' he called, standing up. 'Lucy, I'm here!'

Was shouting the best tactic, given that there were search parties out, scouring the area for the sword? She didn't wave. She was carrying something that was weighing her down. Really, if Col had been thinking straight, he'd have rushed towards her to help with the . . . what was it? What were *they*? Two spades! Over her shoulder, in just the way Col had been carrying the sword. There was something on her back too. Was it a rucksack? He couldn't see.

He waited for her to get closer. She didn't speak, didn't

acknowledge him, until she was near enough to punch him, which, until the very last moment, he thought she might do. Breathing heavily, she dropped the spades. They clattered to the ground. She slipped off the straps of her rucksack. This she lowered more gently.

'Thanks for all the help,' she said. She bent over, hands on her knees. She raised her head. 'And why aren't you at the tower? You know it's over there, right?'

She pointed without looking in the direction of her finger.

Initially all Col could see were pine trees, the brown, the green, the grey. He tried squinting. Still just pine trees. And then the sun blinked from its clouds, and a stream of amber broke like a spotlight down through the branches, and it illuminated . . . a patch of brambles and stinging nettles. But behind these was the tower.

CHAPTER 44

'So the vicar's an absolute legend,' said Lucy. She'd given Col the rucksack but, as a special favour, continued to carry the spades because she'd tried lifting the sword and it was 'bare heavy', and she didn't know how Col managed it, especially not all the way from the church, which was about as long a walk as she'd ever taken because she *really* hated walks.

'Is there anything you don't *really* hate?' asked Col, and it *really* was an effort to get the words out because whatever was in the rucksack was *really* heavy.

Lucy stopped. Lucy thought. 'Sushi,' she said and, as they continued, she explained exactly why the vicar was a legend. She'd called the police, yes, but the storeroom hadn't been raided by a SWAT team. No, a man called Charlie, not in uniform, and who looked too old to be a police officer, had entered with a truncheon, followed by Rosie, to ask what all the fuss was about.

'Draco said it was a lovers' tiff, which was totally gross, and admitted to "accidentally firing an antique pistol". Charlie let me and Dad go, but said that there was a car coming for Draco. He even put her in handcuffs. I don't think he'd heard that she was on the run from the police, what with them discovering all that antique junk after the fire at the castle.'

'But didn't she say anything about the sword?'

'Obviously not.'

'Why *obviously*?'

Lucy sighed like an English teacher explaining how to spell 'onomatopoeia'.

'If the police find out about the sword, it's gone forever. That's why me and Dad kept our mouths shut too. She's devious, Col. She's already escaped from custody once today. I mean, I almost respect her.'

Fear shivered through Col. 'But where's your dad? I thought you said he'd been released.'

'You're crazy for the exposition, aren't you?' said Lucy. Col didn't know what exposition meant, but surely it was fair enough to want to know what had happened. 'He was shot, remember?'

'Like a scratch,' murmured Col.

'Anyway, he helped find the shovels. I've got water and lights too. He said he'd meet us here but, umm, his leg was looking fairly gross, even if the bullet only scraped him.'

The conversation ended. They'd reached the tower. (And its mound.) Or at least *almost* the tower. (And its mound.) Just a few brambles and stinging nettles, rising up from the surrounding weeds, to get through and they'd properly, and finally, be there. They stood shoulder to shoulder, staring up at the ruined structure, the greys and the greens. A butterfly shimmered past. It was the time of day when the light is diffused with magic and, if you'd been there, you'd be pulling out your phone to take a picture.

They had too little time to pose, though. Col sliced with the sword at the mound's bushes, the bushes that stood between them and their destination. The bushes of destiny.

'Because it's totally going to be *so* easy to bury that bad boy, isn't it?' said Lucy, watching him, and, for once, Col totally understood her irony.

CHAPTER
45

'Is this it?' asked Lucy, peering through the trees at the ruined walls of the tower. 'You said it was meant to look like a skull.'

'I think that's the other side?' said Col. (He wasn't sure.)

They stepped through a wall of green leaves. Inside, they could see the structure for what it was. Its footprint was square, about the size of half a tennis court, and, if it ever existed as anything other than a ruin, it might once have had an upstairs. And a roof too. Look up, crane your neck, and glimpses of the heavens could be seen through the ivy, the trees, the grass, past the forest's grasp, those branches desperate to smother the ruined stone.

In the corner were two crushed beer cans, bleached with age. The lower part of the wall behind these was made from breeze blocks, recent repairs to support the structure. On these were lines of graffiti, too faded to read.

Col decided not to tell Lucy about the time he found black candles and an upside-down pentagram chalked here, which his dad had told him had something to do with witchcraft and had given Col nightmares for weeks. The vibes needed to stay positive. Not spooky.

Lucy pointed at a broken garden chair in the centre of the space.

'What if we get disturbed?' she asked. 'Someone's been here before. Someone happy to smash things.'

Col indicated his sword. 'I'll smash them back.'

Lucy looked like she was about to say something scathing, and so, to protect his ego, Col continued quickly with a question.

'Do you think the world will really end if we don't get this done?'

'No,' said Lucy instantly, and I'd be lying if I said Col didn't feel relieved.

'So why are we doing it?'

'Okay, so think of something that means a lot to you,' said Lucy. 'I'm going with my journal.'

'You keep a journal?'

'Yeah, and for your information you're *never* looking at it.'

'Okay,' said Col with a shrug, like this was no big deal, which I'm sure it wasn't.

'When I die, rich and in, like, ninety years, what if I said I wanted the diary buried with me or cremated or whatever? And then what if it wasn't? What if it was put in a museum? What if people, future people, could read it? Wouldn't that be, like, massively invasive and horribly awkward?'

Col nodded in agreement, although he also reasoned that it would partly depend on the journal's contents.

'But this –' and he lifted the weapon a little higher, brushing off some leaves from its blade – 'is a sword.'

'Still,' said Lucy, 'the long-dead warrior wanted it buried with him, not shipped out to Belgium. It's not even like it's going to a museum or to be studied or whatever. Maybe he hated Belgium. Maybe a Belgian man ran off with his wife. How do we know?'

'I guess. Was Belgium around back then?'

Lucy lowered her voice, speaking quickly. 'And returning it might make Dad happy, might . . .' She paused, taking a sideways glance at Col as if she were unsure as to whether she should continue. She did, but her voice was more brittle. 'It might give him time to do other things – you know, *dad* things. With me. Like a regular dad. Like he was before Mum . . .'

As her voice faded, Col felt he should reach out to touch her shoulder, but that would have been the most cringe moment ever, so cringe, in fact, that it alone might have set off the apocalypse. So instead he cleared his throat and said: 'Regular dads aren't all that. I mean—'

But Lucy interrupted him. 'Why are *you* here? Why are *you* helping?'

Col shrugged. 'It's the summer holidays. What else is there to do?'

Lucy picked up the garden chair and threw it past Col. He hoped she didn't notice him flinch. Its plastic smacked against the wall, shattering some more.

'Anyway,' she said, 'we need to dig.'

She positioned her spade, put a foot to it and stabbed it into the ground.

'You've done this before,' said Col, thinking it funny because Lucy *clearly* wasn't into anything that demanded garden tools in any way whatsoever.

'Shut up,' she replied.

CHAPTER
46

You might think that there now follows much description of digging. Well, I'm happy to say that you're wrong. Look at how many pages remain, for one thing. There aren't chapters upon chapters to go, each describing another hour of digging. Think about it. And be thankful. As with *actual* digging, there's only so much description of digging a normal person can take.

This lack of excavatory content isn't due to Col and Lucy's excellent technique, though. They were not great. But, in all fairness, they did their best. A for effort, C for achievement.

It'd be wrong, however, to understate how much digging they did. Because they did **loads**. They also did **loads** of drinking of water from Lucy's rucksack and eating of Mars Bars too, treats that she only remembered she had after much hard work – too much hard work, you might say.

Here's the thing: they weren't quick at excavating soil. Hours passed and there was but a modest pile, and it felt like they'd leaked more sweat than dug earth. They *glowed* heat. If Col's mum could have seen him, she'd have commented on the wonderful effect that activity had on his skin. And she'd be right.

When the sun set, as if frustrated by the amount of time the two of them were taking, they'd turned on Lucy's three camping lamps, positioning them in nooks in the tower walls. The light attracted all kinds of massive, flittering insects, and usually this would have caused Col to freak out, but not now. Because *now* was close to eleven o'clock. Which meant there was only one hour to go before:

THE END OF THE WORLD™.

Lucy's spade caught against something solid, the strike of metal audibly chiming. They froze for a second, both standing in their hole the size of a bathtub. Then Col turned, his shoulders aching more than they'd ever ached, potentially more than any shoulders ever, and Lucy dug down again, and once more she hit something. She dropped the spade and fell to her knees.

'Help me!' she said, and Col did as instructed, not even mentioning his earlier grazes.

They pulled soil from the ground with their hands. Dirt caught under their fingernails, but they didn't care. Why? Because there was something here, and it was hard and wide. And, even in the shadowy moonlight, the material shone like bone. And it had edges, and there was space between these edges, a groove, and then more stone. It was like flagstones you might see in castles or churches, but without the straight lines. It was rougher, as if made by a stonemason in a rush.

Lucy stood and, with the excited buzz of her father, a light and unironic movement of her body that Col hadn't seen before, she used the spade to scrape away the remaining soil. Satisfied that enough was cleared, she edged the corner of the spade into the seam and drew it along, and you'd have thought she was a fully trained archaeologist if you'd seen her. (Although one that, maybe, could have been a little more careful.)

'Look,' she said, standing back and puffing a lock of hair from her eyes. 'I bet if we both wedge our spades in the crack that side, we could lift the thing. I think it's *meant* to be lifted. Like a drain cover.'

Col couldn't help but gulp, thinking of witchcraft (not

drains). He didn't want to free any demons. That'd be bad. He'd have enough problems trying to explain his lost phone to his parents. Regardless, the two took up their positions to the side of the flagstone. Their calves were flush with the soily side of the hole.

'Wiggle it under,' said Lucy. 'Can you feel it? There's space to get your spade in.'

And she was right, but not by much. Col wiggled, then turned to Lucy. She nodded. He wiped some sweat from his forehead, then returned his focus to the spade.

'Now!' she said.

And the two levered their spades and, as easy as opening a wooden trapdoor, the stone shivered upwards. Lucy dropped down, letting go of the spade, to grab the edge. Col quickly did likewise before she could shout at him. It was an awkward position, there was nowhere for his feet to go, so he had to twist his sore knees sideways to make space to lift.

But, and here's the thing, the stone *wasn't* heavy. It was exactly as Lucy had said: designed to be lifted. And so they kept pushing it up and straightening their backs as they went and Lucy let out cheekfuls of air with the effort, but soon they were standing up, and the stone was on its edge, and they gave it one last push, and it fell away to the other side.

A gasp came from the hole, like it was taking a breath. But it wasn't only a hole. At the children's feet, there were steps. And these descended and kept descending until they vanished into inky darkness.

'Off you go, then,' said Lucy. 'I'll stay on guard up here.'

CHAPTER 47

Col held a torch in one hand, the sword in the other. Although he may have looked like a dungeon-crawl character, he very much didn't feel like one.

'When did you first realise you suffered from claustrophobia?' he asked Lucy.

'We don't have time for this,' she replied. 'But, to answer your question, it was today.' Col grunted. He'd suspected as much. 'Remember? When we were almost burned in an underground chamber. And the second time when a gun went off under the graveyard.'

Col checked his sports watch, something he'd tried not to do while digging. It was half eleven.

'What?' The word burst from him in incomprehension. 'Half eleven!' he said to Lucy, showing her the time.

He didn't like the way her face reacted. It was almost like . . . absolute and uncontrollable horror. But the time shouldn't have been surprising. They'd been digging for hours. And look around. The only light was from the torches, and the wood's pine trees seemed to cluster ever closer, grey like pencil drawings.

'Go down, tell me what you see and if you're, like, desperate for assistance, I'll come. I just . . . I'm feeling anxious right now,' said Lucy, in no way sounding anxious.

As she brought her fingernails to her mouth, Col thought, *You're* feeling anxious? but he didn't say anything.

The stone steps were narrow, as if designed for a child. A small child. Col looked at Lucy's feet. His were bigger. But there was no time to argue. He took a step, then stopped. Lucy's hand dropped from her mouth.

'What?' she asked.

'It's just . . . if I don't survive, thank my parents for being –' he struggled for the right word – 'so parent-y. And . . . I don't know if you're into gaming, but you can have my Xbox and games, if you want.'

'Sweet,' said Lucy. 'I'll put them on eBay.' She pointed a finger at the hole. 'I'm joking. Nobody's dying tonight. Now get on with your heroic duty and save the world.'

And if Col felt like crying he didn't show it. And if Lucy noticed that he was shaking she didn't mention it. Instead she watched his slow descent, one step after another, until his head was at her feet and then disappeared into the black.

'Are you okay?' she called.

'I think so!' Col shouted back, a slight echo to his voice. 'The stairs are cold and wet. Like the ones down from the tomb. But they feel older. Like a castle. Medieval maybe.'

'Anglo-Saxon,' she called back.

Entering *this* chamber made Col's chest tighten more than the other two had. Was it the taste of the air, a mustiness like ancient books? Or was it that he was alone now? Or had he played too many games, watched too many films? (Yes.) It felt like the quiet before a boss fight, a new location in which you'd soon get stuck until you either gave up or adjusted the difficulty setting.

'Don't move the stone!' called Col. 'And don't leave me!'

I mean, there was, perhaps, a second's delay before Lucy's response. Was she winding him up, or was she trying to think of the right thing to say? I think the pause was actually – and for once – because she decided to give him a straight answer.

'Don't worry!' she replied. 'I'm going nowhere.'

As Col descended further, the torch's circle of light rolled like a wave. The steps were steep, his head almost brushing against the tight ceiling, and it wasn't until he was almost all the way down that he could see what he was headed towards. For a moment, he was concerned that the steps led to water, that the chamber below was flooded. He was worse at swimming than he was at running and, anyway, could think of few activities more terrifying than doggy-paddling underwater in the pitch-black. But thankfully, both for Col and the world, the only dampness he felt was that of the cold air. (And he could have done with a jacket, to be fair.)

Did the sword feel warm? Was it heating up by increments? It was weird how the mind played tricks like this. He needed a lie-down. He needed a proper meal. A Domino's. His mouth watered. Imagine.

'Please let everything be okay,' he whispered to himself, almost like a prayer, gripping the sword tighter than ever.

And wouldn't it have been sweet if the space into which he stepped was where Conyers was buried? I could imagine now, as I'm writing this, a stone coffin in the centre. The only thing scary about it would be a few cobwebs. There'd be runes carved into the top of the coffin and maybe some Latin too. There'd be a sign and an arrow, indicating where the sword might be deposited. Col would like that. He'd return the sword, he'd skip up the stairs, he'd replace the entrance stone with Lucy and all would be well.

None of this happened because nothing's easy in adventure stories.

The space opened up from the bottom of the steps, but he'd had to duck his head to enter. It was a chamber about the size of Col's bedroom, but there was no bed, no wardrobe, not a single pillow. Much like the entrance stone and the steps down, the slabs that formed the walls and ceiling were a rough mismatch of shapes and sizes, put together by someone with a phobia of straight lines. And, in a very unstonelike way, it didn't feel secure. If Lucy had brought a pogo stick or trampoline, say, and had started bouncing above ground, Col wouldn't have been totally confident that this hole would have continued being a hole.

'Why can't anything be easy?' he whispered, having to make a conscious effort to control his breathing. Hyperventilation would be a bad move. Were there spores down here? Ancient spores that would make him go mad? Away with such thoughts.

He stepped into the centre of the chamber, slipping slightly on the smooth stone underfoot. Pivoting on his heel, but slowly, he turned a full 360 degrees, sweeping the torch round. He saw no skeletons (obviously a good thing). There were no monsters either, no huge serpents that he'd awoken and would now need slaying. Okay. Another positive.

But nor was there an obvious place to put the sword. He swept the torch about again, this time studying the floor. Nothing. But there! A spider! Massive! Scuttling away from the light and disappearing down a crack. Was this only the first part of the burial mound? Would they need to pull open a stone down here too?

He was about to call for Lucy when he noticed it.

CHAPTER 48

A draught.

His first thought was, again, to wish he had a jacket. But the air wasn't coming from the steps. It wafted from the opposite direction. From the wall. Col stepped closer and raised his torch.

At knee-height were three circles of darkness, three holes in the stone. They were large, but not massive. They reminded him of the torpedo tubes he'd once seen on a school trip to Portsmouth. Slightly wider maybe, but definitely big enough to crawl in.

Gulp.

He skidded back across to the stairs, again almost losing his balance. He called up to Lucy.

'There are three holes in the wall! I think, maybe, you're meant to go in one!'

'So what are you waiting for?' she called back.

'You're smaller than me!'

'Get on with it, Col!'

His jaw dropped, but he said nothing. Instead he crossed back to the holes. He thought he should look at his watch, but didn't because that would only make things worse. His heart began to beat faster, and he gripped the sword so tightly his knuckles hurt. And he thought back to the relay race. Immediately, he began to experience that same thickening of the muscles, like concrete was being poured into him, the same slow paralysis of his body.

Not now. Not again. Not here.

The three holes gaped at him. The three holes laughed at him. He'd call to Lucy. He'd tell her he couldn't do it. But not only were his legs frozen, so too was his mouth.

And then Col remembered something. An Xbox game. *Legends of the Sand.* He'd played it last year. There was a part in an early mission that was weirdly similar to this. A choice: one of three. Can you believe it? His mouth popped open. He gasped down air. He'd forgotten to breathe. What an idiot. But it was okay now.

Don't worry about the time. Think about the game. Also, keep breathing.

The mission was underneath a pyramid, not a tower, but there *had* been three tunnels to choose from, and only one led to the pharaoh's treasure, the other two to certain death. And, through a process of trial and error, and dying only a couple of times, he'd chosen the correct tunnel. It had been the right-hand tunnel because left was associated with evil and the middle way was . . . Col couldn't remember what the issue with the central tunnel was, but the trusty, although slightly irritating parrot helping at that stage of the game had definitely explained it to him.

Yes. It would be the right-hand tunnel. He'd never been so sure of anything. *Remember the game. The right-hand tunnel. Excellent. And so to crawl.*

It took some faffing about but, after a few awkward failures, he'd managed to put the torch into the tunnel (and it hadn't revealed anything too scary, only more stone) and then crawled after it headfirst with the sword scraping along next to him, making a horrible sound as it scratched the stone. He couldn't move too quickly because there were only a few centimetres of space round his shoulders and head, and it was like when you see people escape through the air conditioning in action films. But again he told himself that this was fine because in those films you often had henchpeople shooting at the air conditioning, and there was nobody shooting at Col right now.

And it *was* fine: he'd almost convinced himself of this. He only needed to keep moving, a few centimetres at a time, and keep controlling his breathing, and surely the tunnel wouldn't go on for too long, and he could crawl backwards too, he'd already tested this, so he *could* escape, and there was no point thinking about how this must be what it feels like to be buried alive because some people, potholers, actually choose to do this for fun, and maybe focusing on the pain of his knees would help keep panic at the back of his thoughts.

And, yes, he'd almost convinced himself of all this when there was a sudden clattering sound, weirdly like horseshoes against pavement, and it seemed to come from all around him. There was movement ahead – something was falling from the tunnel roof in a rush of cold air. First, it crushed the torch and there was a darkness as total as death, but this wasn't Col's main concern; whatever had smashed the torch had also come down on to the wrist of the hand holding it, and was dead heavy and hurt. His hand was trapped, and he couldn't pull it free.

'No!' was the first word to come from his mouth, and it bounced against whatever was now close to his face and pressing down on his wrist. But it wasn't exactly his wrist that was caught: it was his sports watch. In fact, it had saved his wrist from being completely crushed, had saved him from definite broken bones. What had fallen was stone, straight down like a guillotine blade. It felt smooth, though, and at right angles to the tunnel. Col didn't think there'd been a collapse. This was deliberate. This was designed to crush tomb raiders.

'Help!' he called, with no hope that he was shouting loud enough to be heard on the surface.

He tried pulling out his trapped hand, but it wouldn't come. It was, however, beginning to ache like it'd been struck by a sledgehammer, that dull pain that means something serious has happened.

'*Oh my God, oh my God, oh my God,*' said Col.

It turned out that his knowledge of video games *hadn't* saved him. And, in the utter blackness in front of his face, he thought he saw his parents' faces, and their expressions suggested that they *weren't* angry, only disappointed, and he felt his heart double in weight for the complete mess he'd got himself into.

Still, if they'd believed him about the broadband engineers in the first place, maybe he'd not be here. And if they'd accepted that their son might not like athletics, yes, well . . . he wasn't sure how that would have helped, but it would certainly have improved his general wellbeing.

He gritted his teeth, his mouth turned into a scowl. He no longer worried about explaining what had happened to the iPhone. He'd tell them *everything* when he got home. Then they'd see. *And* they'd believe this time. He'd show them his battle scars.

Col Coleridge, the Boy Who Saved the World.

(*If* ever he got home/saved the world.)

It was as if he didn't make the conscious decision to undo the strap of his watch, to flick his hand away from the fallen stone, before it crushed yet further, flattening the watch. He just did it. And, indeed, he was almost amazed that seconds after thinking about his parents, his hands were free, and he was ready to fight another day.

But they were. And he was.

Col Coleridge, Hero.

(Now without a watch.)

And then suddenly he was being pulled backwards. And fast. He even had to grab at the sword to ensure it came with him. But this was no ancient booby trap. This was Lucy, yanking him, so she thought, to safety.

She came backwards out of the hole, but continued pulling, and Col spilt out into a pile, and the sword clattered alongside him. He rubbed his wrist, wiggled his fingers. Looking up at her, in the glow of the camping lights she'd brought, he hoped she realised how fragile he was. Lucy shook her head with a mixture of affection and desperation, and pointed at the middle tunnel.

'Look!' she said. 'It's the only tunnel with a rune above it.'

'And anyway it's *always* the central tunnel,' she continued. 'Always. Must I teach you everything?'

CHAPTER
49

Col climbed into the central tunnel and pushed another camping light in front of him. He dragged the sword along too, and he swore to himself that this would be the last time he ever did anything like this.

When he reached the distance into the tunnel where he judged the trap to have fallen, he paused and winced. But that was fair enough. He was tired, his knees ached, and he no longer had a sports watch to protect him.

But nothing happened (there was no crushing) so he continued. And when the light toppled away he gasped and suspected another problem – but, no, this was it: mission (almost) accomplished because he could just about see the light ahead shimmering into a new space, a new chamber.

Col flopped headfirst out of the tunnel, wisely leaving the sword behind so as not to have any accidents. He did this in a not particularly graceful way, almost like a baby being born. There was a stranger smell in this part of the tomb, but the floor was still as hard as it had been earlier. The torch had rolled into a corner, so Col couldn't really see what this new place was like, and in particular if there was anywhere obvious to place the sword and so save the world, until he retrieved it.

Which he did. And he could hardly believe what it exposed.

Returning to the tunnel, he pulled out the sword and placed his head in the hole.

'You've got to see this!' he called down to Lucy, his voice rolling along the stone.

Col turned back to take in the room. This *was* unquestionably his destination. The final level. And it wasn't only the carved figure of a resting knight, in a recess at the far end of the room, but also the objects. It was full of shiny things.

Lucy came tumbling out of the tunnel, and Col helped her get to her feet.

'Wow,' she said. 'Who knew warriors had so much stuff? It's like our spare room. Apart from all the gold.'

She pointed to the neat piles of metal plates glistening in the torchlight, the metal goblets that sat next to them. Were they bronze? Copper? Gold, like Lucy said?

There were piles of other stuff too. Wood maybe, broken by the original thief, or otherwise decayed by the passing of centuries.

'Is that a dog?' asked Col, pointing to a small skeleton in the centre of the room. It was surrounded by broken pieces of metal. Had there once been a wooden coffin?

Across from the plates, weapons – obviously weapons – leant against the wall. Enough for a small army. Spears. Swords. Shields. But the metal had corroded, the blades jagged and stained with green, and they looked like they'd shatter if you touched them.

Col lifted his sword. 'Why didn't this rust?'

His question broke Lucy from her trance.

'The sword! We haven't time to gawp. We can Google later.'

And they hurried across the room, dodging the dog out of respect, and came to the resting knight. Or, at least, his statue. His features were clear underneath a sharp helmet. It wasn't that he was smiling, he looked more . . . content. And, droopy moustache aside, he also looked exactly like Lucy's dad, a fact that made them catch each other's eye and smile.

His arms were by his sides. But the hand of the one closest to the edge was clearly sculptured to grip. There was even a groove in the stone that mirrored the sword's shape. This was clearly where it was meant to stay.

Col felt a strange kind of sadness as he returned the falchion, shifting it so that its handle slid into the knight's grip, the length of the blade settling into its indented shape like a fancy piece of modern packaging. It was almost like saying goodbye to a friend. And, the weirdest thing, the cut on his cheek throbbed a little.

He didn't have too long to worry about all this, though. And there was certainly no time to chat with Lucy. For there came a bass rumble, halfway between thunder and an earthquake. Indeed, the stone underfoot seemed to shake. They held out their arms to balance.

'What was that?' asked Lucy.

'I don't know. But I think it wants us to leave.'

'What about all this?' she asked, indicating the room's objects. 'They belong in a museum.'

There came another rumble, louder this time, like the earth was groaning. One of the corroded swords slipped from the wall, shattering as it hit the ground. A stack of plates fell.

'Yes, but so will we if we don't leave.'

Lucy crawled into the hole first, helped into the space by Col. Now there was no mistaking the chamber's vibrations. Even in the tunnel, dust rose in clouds. The camping torch wasn't strong enough to punch through them and so, in some way, it was lucky they had only one direction to go.

Col pulled himself in behind Lucy.

'I don't like this!' she called as the shaking became even more ferocious.

Col closed his eyes, continued pulling himself forward like a tired snake. *Imagine it's an obstacle course*, he told himself. *A primary-school adventure trail. That's fine and not at all terrifying.*

He coughed. Lucy coughed. The dust dried out their mouths. But they continued, falling out of the tunnel into the first chamber, now alight with dust. Lucy stumbled as she headed for the stairs, and Col reached out through the gloom to grab her. It was like being in a storm-shaken ship.

And then up the steps quickly, and ignore the huge cracks that split the stones, and forget that it almost felt like falling upwards because, finally, here was fresh air, dark air, and they were out and into the tower.

Lucy bent double, coughing, the camping light rolling from her feet.

'Keep going!' Col managed to say, pushing at her back.

And she did, and they jumped, shoulder to shoulder, out of the ruined tower. They landed in the middle of a thorn patch and a bunch of stinging nettles, and behind them came a huge cracking and creaking. With a rush of air that sounded like a dragon breathing its last, the tower gave up and collapsed into itself, dust blooming like a raincloud.

Lucy grabbed Col's hand. 'We're still too close,' she said and, pulling him, they half tripped, half jumped out of the brambles and into the trees, falling finally on to a soft patch of dry pine needles.

Their torches were lost but, through the branches above them, there shone a full moon. It was enough to see by, and Col saw that Lucy was smiling, and Lucy saw that Col was smiling too.

'Well,' said Col, 'I guess the world hasn't ended.'

'Shame,' said Lucy. 'That means musicals still exist.'

They laughed.

And, would you believe it, five minutes later they'd both fallen into a deep sleep.

CHAPTER 50

It was the weekend before the new school year. To celebrate, Westerham and Sevenoaks athletics club had organised a charity athletics day. This was different from the earlier *family* athletics day because there was a barbecue, the profits of which went to a local charity for badgers. Also, there was an additional 200-metre race for which you could dress as a clown. If you wanted to.

The Coleridges most certainly did not. Instead they signed up for the family relay again. This time Dad wouldn't have to run twice as Lucy was taking part. And this was all fine with Dr Stones, who watched from the side, because his leg still hurt from, you know, being shot.

In defence of Col's parents, they hadn't pushed their

son to compete. I think the whole 'only son falling through the conservatory roof' had affected them more than they let on. Sometimes you don't realise how precious something is until it falls through a conservatory roof, and you're reminded that it could be lost. But mainly they'd been incredibly impressed with Col's imaginative writing.

With the help of Dr Stones, Col had come up with this fantastical tale of an ancient sword and a flame-haired villain out to steal it. *And* the whole thing was set in Westerham, which Dad very much liked, but Mum worried might alienate people who didn't know the area. Col had wanted to take them to the ruined tower – could even have sent them links to news of Draco's arrest, charged with both graverobbing and smuggling. (Ross and half the gang suffered similar fates.) But Stones had suggested it was best to bury the truth. The tower may have collapsed, but the sword was still down there somewhere. And the fewer who knew that, the better.

Their general good mood, like many people's, also had something to do with the sudden unexpected news that the world's governments had all agreed to a binding climate treaty. And not only that, but leading tech magnates had joined forces to invent a device that could pull carbon from the atmosphere at terrific rates. For once, climate scientists claimed optimism. Imagine that!

And so Col's parents were as close as ever to accepting that his future might not lie in athletics or, indeed, any kind of sport. Still, they hadn't exactly complained when he, on spotting a flyer for the athletics event, suggested the family sign up.

'Thinking of asking that Lucy, eh, son?' said Dad, winking.

Col had smiled when Mum had actually and fully punched her husband.

'Don't be a creep,' she'd warned.

There'd been some discussion as to the order of runners. Dad had insisted he go first. Tactically, this would ensure he built up enough of a lead to give the second runner breathing space. Lucy, because she was new to all this and also not a Coleridge, had been given this spot, therefore, because she'd asked to go second due to 'wanting to get it over and done with before inflicting serious damage on the barbecue'.

And so it came down to whether Mum or Col should take the last place. Given that Col had frozen last time as the *third* runner, it made sense, at least according to Mum, that he should go last.

'Won't that, like, *increase* the pressure?' Lucy had asked.

'We'll be so far ahead by that point that he'll be able to walk to the finishing line, and we'll still win,' Mum had answered. 'No sweat.' She'd giggled to herself. 'I made a joke!'

Reader, it didn't quite work out that way.

With Lucy's dad, in Panama hat, of course, roaring encouragement, Col's dad did as promised. He sped into a commanding lead, almost as if operating with an energy unknown to the other three competitors, two of whom were eight-year-olds.

'Go get 'em, girl!' called Stones from the sideline as Lucy took the baton, and it might have been the absolute cringe of her father's words that caused her to trip. (Or that she was wearing her usual Converse.) But, regardless of the reason, trip she did, a full sprawl that caused onlookers to 'oooh' in sympathy. She was soon up and heading for Col's mum's hand, stretched behind her for the baton as she started to jog, but the lead established by Dad was pretty much gone by now.

Mum made some of it up, and Col began his little jog in preparation for taking the baton, but then – and it happens to professionals, as Mum and Dad repeatedly said afterwards – he mucked up. He was imagining Mum would slip it into his hand as he had the sword into the warrior's. And so he wasn't actually looking at her. Over his shoulder, he was smiling at Lucy. She wasn't hurt – he could see that.

He felt the baton; he started sprinting. But he hadn't properly gripped it. It slipped from his fingers, nearly hitting the ground. He fumbled and caught it at the last moment, but the other families had put their best runners last and, one by one, they overtook him.

And look, the one in the lead, a woman in neon Lycra, was approaching the finishing line, only a few metres away. Col bust his lungs, slicing the air with his hands as he tried to gain on her.

He heard his mum shout, 'It's okay!'

Dad called, 'Don't worry, Col!'

His pace slowed. It *was* fine not to win. It didn't matter. He'd recently saved the world, remember? Give him a break.

And then . . . a plastic bag, as white as a warrior's ghost, drifted across the track and continued drifting . . . until it caught against the lead runner's face . . . which couldn't have been a particularly nice experience. As she tried to pull it off, she stumbled out of her lane and caught the runner alongside her. They bundled to the floor in a heap, exactly in the path of the third runner . . .

. . . who tried hurdling them . . .

. . . but failed.

He collapsed in his own pile of limbs and Lycra.

'Go, Col!' shouted Lucy.

And he did. And at quite a speed. And as long as he reached the line before the others got up he'd win.

Twenty metres.

The Lycra lady was getting to her feet. Come, on Col!

Ten metres.

But she didn't run. She couldn't. She put a hand to her hamstring. Injury!

Col whizzed past. Past her and past the others still on the ground. And he continued whizzing, all the way across the finishing line, as cleanly as a paper aeroplane.

It would have been nice if a huge roar had come from the stands. But there wasn't much of a crowd. Stones clapped, walked over to where a panting Col was being hugged by his parents. Sweating, they finally released their son.

'What an amazing piece of luck,' said Mum. 'That bag! You couldn't make it up!'

'Didn't the sword in your story give you incredible good fortune?' asked Dad.

Standing behind Col's parents, Stones lifted a finger to his lips as Lucy laughed.

'It did,' panted Col. 'What a mad coincidence.'

Acknowledgements

Thanks to Tom Bonnick, my talented, eagle-eyed and brilliantly-named editor. Thank you to Jane Tait for the copyedit, and to Jane Baldock, Kate Clarke, Jasmeet Fyfe, Dan Downham, Juliette Clark, Ellie Curtis, Laura Hutchison and everyone else at HarperCollins Children's Books. Robin Boyden's art work is always fantastic and I'm so lucky to have another of his front covers. Eternal gratitude is deserved by Lauren Abramo, my agent, with whom I've been working for over twenty years (?) now, and her UK equivalent, Anna Carmichael, for her valuable assistance and killer cocktails. Thank you to Dylan, for his help with the book's plotting, and to Jacob for his chats. And thanks too to my wife, Nicky, who understands. Many of the locations of this book exist, including the tower in the woods, and I'd recommend Westerham, Kent, for a Sunday walk with the family!